The Sorcerer's Trap

Novan's country has been conquered, and he is eager to join the freedom fighters. The only trouble is, he's fallen in love with a girl from the other side. When he gets a chance to kill the High Sorcerer, he faces a terrible choice. Soon, he and Alalia are fleeing for their lives.

Fay Sampson is the author of many books for children, teenagers and adults, including the popular Pangur Bán series. She lives with her husband in a centuries-old cottage overlooking Dartmoor, from which she enjoys walking the moors and coast. As well as writing stories of her own, she loves discovering the story of her ancestors' lives.

Also by Fay Sampson:
Pangur Bán, the White Cat
Finnglas of the Horses
Finnglas and the Stones of Choosing
Shape-Shifter: the Naming of Pangur Bán
The Serpent of Senargad
The White Horse is Running
The Christmas Blizzard
THEM

To Lester

THE SORCERER'S TRAP

FAY SAMPSON

LION
CHILDREN'S

A Lion Children's Book
an imprint of
Lion Hudson plc
Mayfield House, 256 Banbury Road,
Oxford OX2 7DH, England
www.lionhudson.com
ISBN 0 7459 4985 1

First edition 2005
10 9 8 7 6 5 4 3 2 1 0

A catalogue record for this book is available
from the British Library

Typeset in 10/13.5 GarmdITC Bk BT
Printed and bound in Great Britain
by Cox and Wyman Ltd, Reading

Chapter One

Novan wiped the sweat from his eyes with a muddy hand. He squinted up from the flower-bed he had been ordered to weed.

A girl, fair as the sun-bleached reeds in the valley below, climbed on to the kerb which surrounded the swimming pool. Tall though she was, Alalia needed this extra height to see over the silvery mesh of the security Fence. She stared to the east, shielding her eyes from the glare. The breeze lifted the dark blue gauze of her robe, so that the silver stars embroidered on it glittered.

The trowel fell still in Novan's hand. For weeks now, Alalia Yekhavu had haunted his dreams, yet she would always be unreachable to someone like him. He ought to hate her.

Squatting down here, Novan could not see what she could. He could not feel the breeze on his sweating face. His rough black eyebrows drew together as he tried to imagine the scene which was meeting her gaze. What must it look like, that coastal plain, the other half of his country, where he had been born? That land she called hers now? She and the rest of the Children of Yadu.

A quiver on his arm, the tickle of tiny feet under his sleeve, made him jump. A pink nose peeped out, followed by a tremble of white whiskers, two astonishingly large black eyes and a pair of cupped ears.

'Do you want to know what she's seeing?' A tiny thread of

5

sound in his mind.

'Get back, Thoughtcatcher!' snapped Novan, startled into speaking aloud. 'Somebody will see you.'

The little jerboa's eyes drew together, seemed to cross, as though focusing beyond immediate time and space on some inner vision. '*She can see a plain reaching away below these hills. Smudged green with a million leaves of orchards in the heat haze. The glimmer of white-walled houses, farms, villages. The flare of red clay tiles. Rich farmland stretching all the way to the distant shimmer of the sea. And one white mountain.*'

'Thanks!' Novan stabbed his trowel into the wet black compost of the flower-bed. He forced himself to keep his bitter thoughts inside his head. 'Thanks for nothing. My land! The land of my grandparents and my great-grandparents, and hundreds more before them. And her lot call it theirs now.'

'*It is theirs,*' returned Thoughtcatcher. '*You lost the war. Remember?*'

'Can I ever forget? Working for them? The Children of Yadu.' The boy threw himself back into his weeding. He wrenched out the unwanted growth and flung the bruised leaves on to the path to shrivel in the sun. Sometimes an exotic flowering plant, brought to perfection in the nursery beds, fell victim to this massacre, along with the native weeds.

'This shouldn't even be my work. The big cats are my job. The leopards.'

He felt Thoughtcatcher scamper into the shelter of his loosely gathered sleeve. When he looked up, Alalia had turned and was looking in his direction, coolly, casually. He longed to know whether she had registered his presence, but she gave no sign. He was just an outdoor servant, one of the conquered Xerappan people, tending the Colony's garden on the Mount of Lemon Trees. If she did notice him, would she recognize him as her leopard-driver?

'Stay out of sight,' he warned Thoughtcatcher.

Jerboas were not uncommon in the dusty hill country of Xerappo. If the Children of Yadu caught a glimpse of one on its own, they would think little of it. But this was different. Jerboas were thought to be shy nocturnal creatures. The sight of Thoughtcatcher tamely crouching by Novan while he worked, still more nestling in his sleeve, would arouse their dangerous curiosity. The Yadu had no idea that the tiny Xerappan jerboas had the gift of reading the thoughts of humans and animals, and could tell them to those they considered friends.

'You're the only advantage we've got, since the Yadu conquered us. You can't save us from suffering and slavery, but you can help us resist them. If the Yadu ever suspected, their sorcerers would exterminate every last one of you.'

'*We have our uses,*' the tiny creature in his sleeve responded modestly.

Unaware that her thoughts were an open secret, should Thoughtcatcher choose to reveal them, Alalia slowly parted the dark blue robe and shrugged it off her shoulders. It revealed a swimsuit and long pale limbs glistening with sun-lotion. She raised her hands above her head and dived into the pool.

The setting on the Mount of Lemon Trees was stunningly beautiful: the cyan-blue pool, its surround painted in brilliant white, broken here and there with an artistically placed black boulder. Palm trees and flowering vines spread a luxuriant backdrop around the walls. They were planted in containers or sunken beds, meticulously watered morning and evening to keep their leaves succulent, their petals vivid. Novan thought of his village at the dusty foot of the hill, and the stream that had once watered its fields. The vines down there were wilting in the heat. The corn was thin and parched.

He felt Thoughtcatcher rubbing the side of his furry little

head against Novan's arm, out of sight, to comfort him. Neither he nor anyone else could hide what they felt from the probing of the jerboa's mind. In dangerous situations, that had sometimes been the only thing which had kept Novan alive.

But today he could not be comforted.

'The Mount of Lemon Trees? It's not even a proper mountain any more. They've flattened the whole peak to make this platform for their colony.'

Raising their roofs against the fierce blue sky, the Yadu houses stretched their shady verandahs along tree-lined avenues. Their gardens were as lush with foliage as the banks of the land's few rivers. '*Ours!*' they shouted. 'This land is ours now.'

And around it all, the shimmering silvery diamond-patterned mesh of the Fence, the Children of Yadu's magical defence against rebellion from below. If Novan glanced sideways at it, dark serpents seemed to writhe through its lighter pattern. He dared not look too closely at them, in case dizziness overwhelmed him and he staggered into their trap.

To touch the Fence was death. Even the Yadu themselves feared it. A lower, solid wall had been built inside the Fence, to protect children or the unwary from straying too close. The lattice had promised to let the colonists see both the plains they came from and the conquered hill country. It was now partially hidden behind something more like a prison wall. Alalia had had to climb on to the kerb around the swimming pool to see over it. Even when the sorcerer sentries passed her through the gate in the Fence, she still needed to be guarded outside. She and the rest of the Yadu.

Childish cries split the noontide air. School was over and the youngsters were rushing to join Alalia in the pool. They ran past Novan without even noticing him.

He straightened his aching neck and looked around him.

Over the wall and Fence he could just see the tops of the other hills which ringed his village below. It was not only the Mount of Lemon Trees. It was every summit: Mount Thunder, Fox Hill, the Mount of Cypresses, the Camel's Back. All flat-topped now, where once there had been natural peaks. All sprouted buildings, shadowed if they faced north, or flashing in the sun from the south. All surrounded by that gleaming, malevolent mesh, which seemed to have a life of its own. The Fence, which kept the conquerors safe and the conquered out.

'Except, of course, that the Yadu need us Xerappans to work for them. So they've got to open their Fence every day and let us in. Somebody's got to water and weed their gardens, sweep their floors, clean their swimming pools, and muck out their animals. Us!'

The shrieks and splashes of the children drowned all other sound. The first warning Novan had that he was not alone in the flower-beds was the boot which toppled him face forward on to the dark earth.

'You can keep your dirty eyes off Yadu girls in swimsuits.'

Novan felt a sweat break out that was colder than the perspiration of hard labour. He got back on to his knees and turned. There was soil in his mouth which it was too dangerous to spit out yet, lest that should seem like an insult. He lowered his lids over the resentment flashing in his eyes. He must discipline himself not to show the fury he was feeling... and the guilt. He *had* been watching Alalia.

He saw the lower folds of a tunic, the dark plum-red uniform of the Sorcerer Guard. A pair of elegantly pointed boots. This had been no brutal kick. The wearer of the boots had applied only a light prod at the exact spot calculated to send Novan tumbling off balance.

Slowly, keeping his anger under control, Novan allowed his gaze to travel higher. He tried not to flinch at the sight of the spell-rod, half hidden in its leather sheath. He made himself concentrate instead on a tall and slender form under the loose, light tunic. A pair of narrow shoulders with the green epaulettes of a probationer guard. A fair, pointed face, glistening with the same sun-lotion as the girls in the pool. The same thin, fine hair falling almost to his shoulders. Dark sunglasses hid his eyes. It was Alalia Yekhavu's elder brother, Balgo.

'She's not for you.' The voice was quiet, relishing an authority that had no need to shout to assert its power. They both knew this. Novan said nothing, but surreptitiously wiped his gritty tongue on the back of his hand.

'Don't let me find you playing Peeping Tom again.' Softer, and yet more menacing.

'No, sir.' There was no point in explaining that weeding the swimming-pool garden was not his choice. That he had finished cleaning the leopards' cage and the estate manager had sent him here to do this job. Balgo must have known that.

The Yadu youth strolled away down the path, flicking the leaves of scented bushes. Novan began to gather up the weeds. He found he was trembling. At last, viciously, he could spit the dirt from his mouth.

A girl's cry echoed from the walled pool. 'Alalia! Is it true what they're saying? You're going to be engaged?'

A gasp broke from Novan. Amid the shouts and laughter which greeted this question, he could not make out Alalia's reply distinctly.

There was a whisper in his mind, from his sleeve edge. *'She's going back to the land of Yadu. To Femarrat, the sacred mountain, to be betrothed to Lieutenant Digonez of the Sorcerer Guard. Lord Cozuman's own nephew. Her family have high hopes of this marriage.'*

'What's that to me?' murmured Novan savagely.

'Everything, I should have thought,' came the reply.

Chapter Two

At sunset, when the Fence was opened to let the workers out, there were only random searches. It was what the Xerappans might bring in with them in the morning that the Yadu feared. Among the anonymous, seemingly obedient workforce there might be a saboteur, a terrorist. Xerappans did not have the high magic of the Children of Yadu, but they were said to have secret knowledge of more contemptible means, like poisons. Easy to conceal. It made the guards nervous.

Tonight, however, there was no need for Novan to set Thoughtcatcher down to make his own furtive way through the gap in the Fence. It was unlikely that Novan would be pulled out of the queue to be frisked for stolen articles. And if he were, the jerboa would sense the guard's intention in time to escape.

Suddenly Novan flinched. Alalia's brother was on duty at the Fence. At least Balgo did not look quite as scornfully proud of his status here. He was only a probationer guard, in his first year of service after training. He would not, of course, be in charge of opening the Fence for so large a number. He stood a little to the side, one step back from the Sergeant Sorcerer with the blue epaulettes. Every so often, at the sergeant's word, he hauled someone aside and searched them. A female probationer on the other side did the same with the women.

'I hate this bit,' muttered Oniron, the lion groom.

'Me too.' Novan still kept his eye on Balgo.

There was always this tension. However often he went through, however rarely he was singled out, the possibility remained. He must stay alert, ready for that swift, panic-inducing signal from Thoughtcatcher, who was now clinging out of sight inside his trouser leg. The jerboa would be out in a flash. His long thin hind legs would propel him swiftly among the mass of boots, sandals and bare feet beyond the Fence. Then he would wait for Novan in the scant shelter of weeds beside the road.

The column of workers approached the gap in the black inner wall. The sergeant unhooked the rod from his belt. The sight of it always made Novan go cold. The sorcerer's rod looked so small, so simple, almost elegant. A smooth, white cylinder, slimmer than his wrist, the ends capped with gold. But in trained hands, its power could be terrifying.

The sorcerer pointed it at the unbroken silver mesh barring the road. Novan always strained to hear what the sentry said, but in nearly two years of working inside the Colony he had never yet been able to make out the words. It did not seem to matter how close he got to the head of the queue, how loudly the sentry spoke. There was something in the quality of the very words of the spell. No one could catch them who had not been inducted as a sorcerer. They could not be remembered and used by anyone unauthorized. Not even Thoughtcatcher could tell him what they were. It was no wonder that members of the Sorcerer Guard looked arrogant.

The air shimmered. The sun was making scarlet banners of low cloud on the western horizon, yet the light at the front of the queue shone brighter than noonday. It was hard to watch, as it had been hard to listen. But slowly, sinuously, like a troupe of silver-clad dancers, sections of the Fence drew apart, refigured their pattern and opened up a way into the evening air that was reddening the road down the hill.

12

'Shift it.'

Novan edged forward, with Oniron behind him. There was a prickle that was on the verge of pain. He was outside the Fence.

He still felt this sense of relief every time he stepped beyond the barrier. The Colony's estate extended on down the hill to the outskirts of Novan's village. But from here on, nothing separated Yadu land from Xerappan other than an ordinary drystone field wall. The difference was in the colour of those fields. Tall healthy vines, lush melons and squashes, lemon-tree orchards on the upper side. Below, around his village, a mutilated land. Ancient trees had been ripped out, so that they could not provide shelter within range of the road for rebellious boys armed with stones and catapults. Fields of beans and lettuces looked dejected and dry, barely kept alive by the dwindling stream. The Yadu had diverted the head waters to irrigate their own fields.

Novan was too tired and numbed to feel anger at this contrast every day. The Xerappans had lost. The Yadu were taking more of their land month by month. There was nothing they could do.

Light feet came running down the track behind them, overtaking older workers trudging homeward. A skitter of little stones bouncing past him announced the arrival of his sister Mina. Novan turned with a half-smile.

She was smaller than he was, yet with the same compact and sturdy build. Her eyebrows were dark like his, but the skin of her face was paler. Mina worked indoors, for Alalia Yekhavu's family. Her bare feet padded on cool marble floors, while her brother sweated among the animals. Her arms ached, like his, from washing and polishing, but to be a house servant was something of a privileged status. Alalia occasionally spoke to her as if she were a human being. Novan's pride was in his leopards.

13

'Hang on,' she called.

The sun was dipping below the hills, leaving a cooler twilight. Mina stopped and lifted the hem of her long dress. There was a band of cloth stitched around the inside. The seam was hidden on the outer side by a wide border of embroidery. From this hidden pocket she gently lifted her own jerboa. Where Thoughtcatcher's was the typical grey-brown, like a mouse, Whisper's fur was an unusual white, patched with black. The cups of her alert ears showed pink, almost translucent. Mina set her down on the path.

Thoughtcatcher slipped from the gathered cuff of Novan's trouser leg. The two little creatures nuzzled noses, twitching their whiskers. No doubt there were reams of intelligence passing between them, but the humans could not hear it. Relieved from the glare of the sun, the jerboas' black eyes widened. They scampered off the track to bound through the wayside weeds. Hind legs, longer than their bodies, sprang them in joyful leaps after the day's cramped hiding.

Mina was humming.

'What are you sounding so pleased about?'

'Guess.'

'Alalia's given you one of her old dresses.' But Mina was not carrying anything, and the guards would have questioned her if she had been.

'Nope.'

'Mrs Yekhavu has at last noticed that furniture doesn't polish itself and said thank you.'

'That'll be the day.'

'What then?'

'Not telling till we get home.'

He looked at her fondly. She was twelve. She shouldn't be working from sunrise to sunset for insulting wages. She should be in school, like those Yadu girls who had come running out to dive into the pool. But what choice did she have, any more than he had? They were not exactly slaves, but the little they earned was what lay between them and starvation. The Yadu had devastated their grandparents' farm. It could hardly support the old couple, let alone all their dispossessed relations who had fled from the east. The Xerappans were losers. Novan was not going to slap Mina down if she had found something to smile about.

The colours around them changed. They were passing out of the Colony's lemon orchards, with their glossy deep-green leaves, into the dusty brown of the Xerappan village. There were sentries at this boundary too, with sorcerers' rods clipped to their belts, but they were more casual than those at the Fence. They watched the homegoing workers with little curiosity. The two jerboas bounded freely past them, almost invisible in the deepening shadows.

'Wait!' Novan checked Mina abruptly, out of earshot of the guards.

Something had tipped his softening mood back to anger. Just below the orchard wall a natural terrace of rock overlooked the road. Once a house had stood here. Its foundation courses of rough-hewn stone were still clearly visible. Novan's old home. The house his parents had built after the war had sent them fleeing westward as refugees, back here to his mother's village. The house that had been his home as a frightened child. Where Mina was born.

But it had not been enough for Yadu sorcery to win the war. They had pursued the refugees westward, deep into Xerappan territory. They had seized the hilltops and planted their colonies on them. Novan and Mina's home had been too close to the road, too easy for a rebel to hide in and launch some pathetic weapon at the passing Yadu. The sorcerers had destroyed it.

Novan glanced over his shoulder. The sentries could see him if they turned, but what did he care? He leaped up on to the platform and stood in what had once been his mother's kitchen. He raised his fists against the sunset sky. He wanted to yell out defiance, but that was too much to dare. One day, *one day*, he would find a way to strike back.

'Come down!' Mina was hissing. 'They'll see you. They could strike you with a felling-spell from where they're standing.'

'You think I don't know that?'

But he slipped down into a sitting position on the lip of the terrace and let himself drop into the dry grass below. She was right. There was no point in throwing his life away. He would fight for Xerappo, die for his suffering country if necessary, but he would need to be clever, secretive. He must find a way under their powerful magic to where it would hurt them most.

They made their way on in silence. The twilight was cool, still faintly scented with lemon. The wide column of workers which had trudged down the road was breaking up, individuals trickling away to their separate houses.

'See you.' Oniron waved goodnight.

Mina and Novan turned aside from the main track and took a narrower path through the scrub to a low farmhouse.

It was old, with rough stone walls, not plastered or whitewashed. Some tiles had slipped on the roof. They would need to be mended before the winter rains came. A subdued lamplight showed through the windows.

The living room seemed full even before they entered. Their mother, a big, strong woman with severely straight hair, was stirring a pot on the stove. Their father, seated ready for the meal, was smaller. He seemed to have shrunk from the strong man Novan remembered from his childhood, as though height and flesh had been taken away from him, along with his dignity, when he became a refugee. Novan's mother's parents, Luella and Tiaman, were busy about the table. They were two spry spare old people. They hardly seemed big enough between them to have produced such a large woman as Novan's mother. This was their home, overwhelmed now by the increased family.

Two other old people sat in the shadow, listless, defeated. His father's parents. Grandfather Elyas and Grandmother Roann had fled with them from their own home in the east. That was the fertile half of the country, now renamed Yadu. It was the coastal plain which Alalia had been looking at when she stood on the wall. This couple had lost everything: home, land, income, self-respect. They had found refuge in the home of their daughter-in-law's parents, on a farm that could now barely sustain its owners. The village of Thornycreek might lie in conquered territory, overlooked by half a dozen Yadu colonies, but, for now at least, this was still the land of Xerappo.

Grandmother Roann still wore at her belt the heavy iron key which fitted the door of her lost home. Novan did not need to peer across the lamplight to know that her knotted fingers would be twisting it on her lap. She would never forget her loss.

There was a meeting of jerboas, the tiniest twitter of cries.

Mother heaved the pan of beans on to the table. 'Wash your hands and come to supper, before we all fall asleep in our chairs.'

But Mina could not eat, even when she had the spoon in her fist. She was drumming the end of it on the table top in her excitement. 'Guess what?' she burst out.

Faces turned to her, caught in the golden circle of the lamplight. She looked round at them expectantly.

'Spit it out, then,' smiled her father. 'Don't keep us in suspense. You're dying to tell us.'

'Alalia Yekhavu is getting engaged.'

'So what's new?' muttered Novan. 'She's going to be

17

betrothed to Digonez, Lieutenant of the Sorcerer Guard.'

'You knew?' Mina was momentarily taken aback. 'But they only announced it today.'

'It didn't take long for it to get around the swimming pool.'

'Bet you don't know where the betrothal ceremony's taking place.'

'Mount Femarrat. The sacred mountain.'

Mina threw down her spoon in frustration.

'Go on,' prompted her father. 'It must be more than that to make you so excited. So the young lady you work for is going away to be betrothed to the High Sorcerer's nephew, and...?'

'And I'm going with her. She's asked for me to go as her personal maid.'

There was the gasp of surprise that she had hoped for, and a little cry of pain from Grandmother Roann. Grandfather Elyas reached out his hand and gripped hers.

Femarrat, the white mountain that rose out of the plain close to the sea. Not ten miles from the farm to which Grandmother still had the key. Femarrat, holy to the Xerappans for thousands of years, but to the Yadu too, so they claimed. Their sacred stories twined like serpents, rivals for this beloved place.

'I never thought I'd ever go to Femarrat.'

The stories their grandparents told Novan and Mina about the mountain had fired them both with longing. Now, against all expectation, Mina was going to set foot on it. She, alone of all of them.

Novan tore his hunk of bread apart in a spasm of jealous rage.

Chapter Three

Grandfather Elyas crumbled bread between his fingers. There was a faraway look in his eyes.

'Mount Femarrat. I can't explain to you young ones what that means to us. As though the land had risen up out of the earth and come alive. Come to meet us. Just as if we were little children playing round our mother's knees. We *loved* that mountain.'

'We were married there,' said Grandmother Roann dreamily.

Elyas put out his hand and covered hers. 'We all were, in those days. Your parents too, when they were not much older than you are, Novan. We set out in two processions to climb the mountain. Oh, not to the very top! The Yadu have no idea. That peak used to soar into the sky, like a white bird climbing to heaven. They tell me the idiots have knocked the top clean off it, and built their own temple there instead.'

'It's true,' said Novan's father. 'Word came to us that Lord Cozuman has made a platform up there. Just like the ones they build their colonies on here, only higher. And they've hauled black stone all the way up the mountain, to build something that should never be there by nature. You can see it for miles around.'

'It's what he always does,' Grandfather's voice was sharp with sorrow. 'Power. He wants everyone to see they're on top, and we're nothing. His black temple in place of our white mountain top.'

'They say it's *their* sacred mountain,' said Grandmother Roann in a low voice.

'Rubbish! What do they know about it? Thinking the top of it's the most sacred place, for a start. They don't understand that was always the head, not the heart of it.' He let the silence lengthen.

'No. We learned that on our wedding day. There were two processions started out: one for the bridegroom, one for the bride. But we went different ways. Mine climbed rightwards, hers went left. Between us we circled that mountain, going always higher, or so we thought. Until we came to a place where it seemed the mountain had fallen in on itself. It was a deep, dark hollow, with water at the bottom. You came down from the blinding sun and the white rock into the dark, cool shadow of trees. It did something to you, standing there in the shade by that pool. You felt the blessing, like there were kind arms round you, wishing you well. Something you'd never feel on any mountain top, in the heat of the sun.

'I felt small, and she was very great. The mountain, I mean. And yet she loved me.

'And then my Roann came.' Grandmother looked up and smiled at him. 'Only I didn't recognize her at first. This is the bit I still don't understand. They'd dressed her like they dressed all brides on Mount Femarrat, in a wig of flax. So all her black hair had turned to pale gold... just as if she'd been a Yadu woman! Only I didn't think that at the time, of course, because they were still far away across the sea. It's always puzzled me. Nobody could tell me why we did that. Just that it had always been done. That Xerappan bridegrooms were always dark, or if a few of them weren't by nature they coloured them with soot. And the brides were always made out to be fair.' He shook his head.

'But there was something else that made us feel we were

on the edge of a mystery. There were holy people there, singing songs for us and plucking the strings of their lyres. And the Chief Guardian of them, a woman it was, put a garland of flowers round both our necks and led us down into the pool.

'I say "down", and I mean it. We could feel the ground shelving away under our feet with every step we took into the water. It was getting deeper and deeper, till I thought she was going to lead us right under. Only we stopped when it was waist-deep. And then she threw the water over us, as if that would do instead of drowning us. And everybody laughed and cheered. And she told me I could kiss the bride.' He smiled back at Roann. 'I couldn't wait to get that fair wig off her head and see her as she really was.

'Only... it's a funny thing. When that Chief Guardian led us back out of the water, I felt I didn't want to go. It was as though that pool was pulling me. As though it really meant for me to go deeper. As though there was something it wanted to show me.

'So that's why I think those Children of Yadu have got it all wrong. Knocking off the peak of the mountain and putting that temple up there. As if that was the way they could get power over it and make it theirs.' He shook his head, still struggling to understand.

'The secret's not up there. It's deeper down. I sometimes wonder... if I'd had the courage to go deeper into that water, to go under it, what might I have found down there? I've a feeling the truth of it all is in the heart of that mountain.'

'The Jerboas' Nest.'

The thread of thought startled them. It was several moments before they looked away from Grandfather Elyas to search for the source of it on the hearthrug. Thoughtcatcher's eyes shone in the firelight.

'That's what we call it. Mount Femarrat is sacred to us

jerboas too, you know. And Whisper is going there.'

Novan turned to look at Mina's jerboa. She was washing her black-and-white nose with a tiny paw, shyly. Her round black eyes looked enormous.

'Well, whatever the secret of Mount Femarrat was,' Novan's father said bitterly, 'it's lost to us now. Cozuman killed the Chief Guardian and all her followers.'

Chapter Four

Behind the railings of their compound, the leopards moved as though through the barred shadows of woodland. Their spotted pelts rippled over the flow of powerful muscles. Paler gold than the brilliant sunshine, patterned blacker than the deepest shade. Stealthy paws, their claws sheathed, scarcely disturbed the red sand. One, whom Novan had named Almond, lay along the limb of a tree, barely discernible, for all her size, in the dappled leaf-shadow. Only her tail, with its upcurved tip, hung clear, twitching gently.

Novan saw them start when the buckets clanked as he set them down before the gate. This was always a nerve-wracking moment. Behind him was Balgo. The probationer sorcerer's rod was unclipped from his belt, ready to strike a spell if Novan made one false move. In front of him, when he opened the gate, would be a dozen deadly animals waiting their moment of revenge on the humans who had caged them here.

'Get on with it. That's not the only work you've got to do.' Balgo's snapped command told that he was tense too.

Novan felt Thoughtcatcher twitch in his trouser leg, where the baggy cloth was gathered in at the ankle.

The gate swung stiffly inwards against the resistance of its springs. There was the softness of sand under Novan's soles. The leopards had stiffened, in a half-circle now. Almond, the animal in the tree, slithered down to join them. They were staring at him, at the buckets of food. He had to will himself across the space to the empty troughs. The leopards were willing themselves too to stay still, at a prudent distance.

Just for a moment pride flared through Novan. None of the Yadu would have dared to make this walk into the compound, not even Balgo with his sorcerer's rod. The leopards would have attacked them without hesitation. The magic of a sorcerer's rod could stun or kill them, but it could not tame them.

His arrogance ebbed away. It was not him the leopards were afraid of. He could do nothing alone.

He came within their semicircle and felt in his own nerves the shudder he saw run through them. Their amber eyes were staring, not into his face, but towards his ankle. Novan was seized with a new alarm. Couldn't the Yadu see? Did they never suspect? Surely they must know by now that there was nothing in the Xerappans for human or beast to be afraid of? The leopards knew where the real power was, and they trembled. They did not need to see Thoughtcatcher and his friends. The mere presence of a little jerboa was enough to hold them in quivering docility.

He filled their feeding troughs and checked that their drinking pool in the shade was being replenished with a constant flow of water. Then he went back to force the gate open again and drag in joints of meat.

While his back was turned, the big cats had closed in on wary feet to the softer food in the troughs, but they lifted eager eyes to the sight of flesh and bone. Shivers of longing ran under their skin. Novan tried not to meet their stares, to forget that he was flesh and bone too. Thoughtcatcher's fur tickled his shin. He felt comforted.

He was scarcely back at the gate before the leopards were released from their trance. They leaped on the bloody joints and began to tear them from each other.

Novan was trembling himself as he bolted the heavy gate behind him. Balgo could have relaxed now, moved off. But the tall Yadu youth stood staring curiously at Novan.

'How do you do that? Scare the leopards into obeying you? And lions too? You don't know anything about magic, your lot. You'd never have let us walk all over you in the war if you did. So what is it with the animals?'

Novan shrugged. 'Just a gift, I suppose. Like some people are good at singing.'

'Just as well for you, since there's something in your wretched climate which makes our horses sicken and die out here, and you can hardly expect a camel to pull a chariot. And my mother's rather proud of her leopards. You have your uses.'

The Xerappan boy stood silent, head bowed, letting the weight of the empty buckets seem to bow his shoulders.

Balgo walked all round him, inspecting him. Novan was terrified the guard must see the slight bulge in the folds of his trouser leg, where Thoughtcatcher crouched.

'We'll have to smarten you up if you're coming east with us.'

The shorter boy's head jerked up, eyes suddenly questioning.

'Oh, don't pretend you didn't know,' Balgo laughed. 'My sister's getting herself betrothed. And since her intended is the High Sorcerer's nephew, the ceremony will be back in Yadu itself, at the temple on the summit of Mount Femarrat.'

What's that to do with me? Novan wanted to shout.

'Leopards, sonny,' said Balgo, as though he could read his face. 'My sister will need four leopards to draw her chariot in style, as well as lions for the baggage carts she's sure to need. Unfortunately, that means we shall have to take some Xerappans along too. You, for instance.'

'To Femarrat?' Stupid with astonishment.

'All the way. And you'd better be on your *very* best behaviour inside our homeland.'

The words reeled through Novan's mind. For hours he had lain awake last night envying Mina. She was going back to what had once been the sacred heart of Xerappan country. To a mountain she had never seen, but in the shadow of which their father's family had their roots. Where Novan had been born. A land normally forbidden now to Xerappans from this side of the hills. Novan's short life had been bitter with the belief that he could never go back there. He had plotted ridiculous schemes of resistance fighting or subterfuge which would take him across the border from occupied Xerappo into Yadu itself. Now, without him lifting a finger, it was happening.

Alalia was getting engaged, to someone else. It could never have been otherwise, of course. But out of the bitter shattering of one impossible dream came this other unlooked-for granting of a very different wish. He would go to Femarrat as a forced labourer in Alalia's household. He would be her groom, not her bridegroom. He would tame leopards and lions for her. She would hardly notice him.

But he would stand on the sacred mountain.

'Once,' Novan said to Oniron, as they munched their bread and cheese under the olive branches, 'once we were the greatest country in the world. People came to Mount Femarrat from hundreds of miles away to bring us tribute. Even the Yadu from their islands in the Eastern Sea. My granddad says they sent ships loaded with gold and diamonds. Elephants came from the south bringing ivory and spices. Camels from the Western Desert with carpets and copperware. There were furs of wolves and bears from the north...'

'Yeah. That was then,' said Oniron. 'It isn't going to happen again, is it? The Yadu have got everything now. Even us.'

'Not me!' Novan hurled an olive stone with all his force into the bushes. At once, the two of them looked round with alarm, in case one of the guards had heard and drawn his rod. Even the slightest gesture would be taken as hostile.

'You see?' said Oniron. 'Nothing we do is safe. We're in their power.'

'There has to be a way,' Novan muttered, hating himself for his show of fear. 'There has to be a way for us to be free.'

Chapter Five

The evening before their departure Novan groomed the leopards, rubbing their short, dense coats with a silken cloth. He felt them trembling at his touch. Low growls thrummed through the twilit air. Their tails twitched. When he had first been taught this work, a little part of his mind had wondered if they might actually be enjoying his stroking. He thought their growls were colossal purrs. Now he knew the truth: leopards don't purr like domestic cats. His life depended on taking nothing for granted. The leopards, the Yadu; one unwary step and there would be no time for questions.

Just now, as so often, he owed his life to a little jerboa. Thoughtcatcher was in his left sleeve today, cradled at the elbow as in a hammock. Novan's left hand held the big cat steady, while his right hand worked rhythmically. This was one of the larger males, Quercus. It was good to feel the warmth of the little rodent.

Thoughtcatcher was not communicating with Novan now. All his mind was fixed on this leopard, who could eat him in a mouthful, and on the rest of the leopards watching. His tiny brain was subduing their far larger ones. A sudden thought chilled Novan's blood. How long did jerboas live? What if Thoughtcatcher died, here in the leopards' pen? It would be all over for Novan in minutes as they tore him apart, but that wouldn't be quickly enough.

He was trembling himself now, and he had to stop the

grooming. Quercus's growl was rising; he was starting to get to his feet. Novan could almost feel Thoughtcatcher's concentration screaming through the atmosphere as he fought to regain control. The leopard dropped to his belly and rolled over in the sand, undoing Novan's careful brushing.

The leopards had hardly needed grooming. They kept themselves sleekly elegant. But Alalia had ordered it for her betrothal procession, just as Mina said she had set going a whirlwind of designing and cutting and stitching for a whole new wardrobe of clothes. And Novan had not objected. The leopards were his pride. No one else had the same sureness of touch, such deep understanding of them, thanks to Thoughtcatcher. It was only a pity he had to make them ready the night before, when they might mess their burnished coats while they slept. But the convoy must leave early tomorrow, by starlight, to travel as far as they could in the cool of the morning.

A sorcerer let him out of the cage and he went to help Oniron next door.

The lions were another matter. They seemed big, shambling brutes after the flowing grace of the leopards. Oniron was hard at work on them. Novan caught his look of relief at having not only a second jerboa to help his, but one as famed as Thoughtcatcher. The boys worked faster now. Night was approaching. The males were the hardest, with their coarse, tangled manes.

'They're only going to be pulling the baggage carts, for goodness' sake,' Oniron complained. 'Why do we have to get them brushed like brand-new carpets?'

'Pride,' said Novan. It had a double meaning for him. Yes, Alalia Yekhavu was proud, and wanted everyone back in the land of Yadu to know that her family had done well in their Xerappan colony. Her father was governor of the Mount of

Lemon Trees. She was no mean catch, even for a lieutenant of the Sorcerer Guard at the High Command of Femarrat. But Digonez was Lord Cozuman's nephew. The fear of the High Sorcerer's name subdued even the Children of Yadu. Alalia was making a brave, bold bid for self-respect.

But Novan was proud too, proud of the big cats, proud of his skill with them. That, and nothing else, had won him a place on this momentous journey into Yadu.

By the time they had finished, down to the tip of the last lioness's tail, it was almost too dark to see the golden glow of their labours. The other workers had long since passed through the Fence and were resting their weary bodies over the supper table. It was eerie walking along the deserted paths of the Colony, with the shade trees blackening the air in advance of night. Across the gardens, lights shone in the Yadu houses. There was chatter and laughter of people enjoying the cool of evening, the smell of delicious food. The boys said little to each other, and in low voices. One suspicious sound, and death might flash from a house as they passed. In Xerappo, the Yadu were always jumpy. Even inside their Fence they never seemed quite relaxed.

The Xerappan boys were not, of course, alone. A little distance behind them they could hear the footsteps of the guard escorting them, whose name Novan could not remember. Even the space the sorcerer left between him and them was ominous. A slay-spell from one of those houses could fell the boys and leave him untouched. To be a Xerappan was to be permanently in danger. Both boys knew that their jerboas were alert, straining to give them that split-second warning which might make the difference between life and death. Though with the guard directly behind them, a first failed spell would be immediately followed by a more final second one.

Don't get angry, Novan told himself. There's nothing you

can do. Yet.

The Fence shimmered in the almost-darkness. There was a sentry waiting. It was too dark to see the colour of her epaulettes, but Novan judged by her build, rather short for a Child of Yadu, that it was probably Private Genadda. An officer was only essential when the big crowds passed through, morning and evening.

'The cat grooms,' called the escort from behind them. 'All above board. Special duties preparing for Alalia Yekhavu's convoy tomorrow.'

'They'd better be quick if they want some sleep, then,' laughed Genadda. 'She's leaving at four in the morning. They'll need to be back to harness the cats by three.'

It was always both fearful and magical, the opening of the Fence to let them out. It was as though the stars themselves gathered together and then parted to reveal a river of darkness. Novan plunged out into it with a feeling of relief and freedom. No one had searched them. The moment they were outside, the jerboas leaped from their hiding places and were dancing for joy in the night. Novan and Oniron could not see them, but heard faint squeaks of ecstasy, now on one side of the track, now impossibly far on the other side, as their powerful hind legs uncramped themselves at last.

'Let's run,' said Oniron. 'I'm starving.'

It was crazy, dangerous, racing steeply downhill over the uneven track with its loose stones. Back in Yadu, Novan had been told, there would be proper roads, where chariots and carts could roll smoothly for mile after mile. Already the Yadu were planning to build such roads to connect their scattered colonies in the land of Xerappo. But not, it was rumoured, for Xerappans to use.

Never mind. He was going to Yadu. He would see their roads and their towns. He would see his own birthplace. It would be heartache and joy at the same time. He would see

31

what he had lost.

He would be driving Alalia.

The family were all clustered around the table. They had finished eating, but Novan sensed the moment he entered that they had been talking about him.

'Go to bed, Mina,' said his mother, almost as soon as they had greeted him. 'You've got a big day tomorrow, and a very early start.'

'So's Novan. And it'll be ages before he's ready for bed yet.'

'No reason for you to lose your beauty sleep, just because they make him work all hours of the night.'

'Work! You should have been at the Yekhavus' house. It was bedlam. Washing her hair. Packing her clothes, and we mustn't get the slightest crease in the wrong place. And the perfumes and the creams and the bath oils she's ordered. As if there won't be far more beauty shops where we're going. And yet she complains it cost twice as much to have them sent out here.'

'First impressions. Your young lady wants her fiancé to see her at her best, even before you've got her ready for her betrothal ceremony.'

'He's seen her already, hasn't he? Though I suppose it *was* two years ago. She'll have grown up a bit since then.'

'Stop chattering,' their father put in. 'Do as your mother says. Here's Novan dying for his supper, not girls' gossip.'

Novan's mother jumped. 'I'm sorry, dear. You must be hungry, as well as worn out. I've saved a big bowl of stew for you.'

'I'm almost too tired to eat.'

But he sat down, because it was less trouble to do as he was told than argue with her. And once he lifted the first spoonful to his mouth he realized he was ravenous. Yet by the time he had finished, his head was drooping towards the table. Dimly he was aware of Grandfather Elyas's voice at his elbow, low, urgent.

'Novan? Are you listening?'

With an effort he pulled himself up straighter, trying to make his blurred eyes focus. Grandfather was pushing something against his hand. It was hard to see what it was. A very small, slender packet, which seemed to be wrapped in thin skin.

'We daren't give you much,' Grandfather murmured. 'You're bound to be searched. But your grandmother can sew this into the collar of your shirt. They shouldn't be able to feel this amount under the braid and embroidery. Even a little can be deadly, if you pick the right opportunity.'

Novan was aware of the cool, smooth casing alongside his fingers. He felt a great resistance to lifting his hand and taking it. And yet he was fascinated, half knowing, half fearing.

'What is it?'

'Grommalan.'

There was the sound of sucked breath around the room. Even Grandfather Elyas looked at the door as he spoke, as though he feared an informer might be listening. Grommalan was their most potent poison.

'W-what am I supposed to do with it?'

As he spoke, he was powerfully aware that somebody was standing behind him. Could he have come in while Novan had been drowsing over his supper, or had he been in the shadows all the time?

Novan turned. The man was big, very big for a Xerappan. A loose brown robe enveloped him from shoulders to feet. His head was wrapped in a yellow scarf that showed only his eyes. They burned with a dark intensity.

The man put out a large, blunt hand and rested it on Novan's shoulder. The boy shuddered, as the leopards did when he touched them.

'I think you know.' The voice was powerful with authority, though low and muffled.

Thoughts raced through Novan's mind. All his boyhood he had dreamed of resistance. He had been the hero, striking out against the conquering Children of Yadu. A freedom fighter.

Now his moment had come. He was going into the heart of Yadu, to Mount Femarrat, the headquarters of the Sorcerer Guard. There would never be another opportunity like this.

But grommalan. He had not imagined this, though he knew now that he should have. Of course catapulted stones could never achieve anything. He had longed for a spear, a scimitar, a galloping horse. Yet ordinary warfare could do no good against the spells of sorcerers' rods. And the Xerappans had no magic of their own to match the Yadu's. So it had to be poison. It was the only weapon the underground had. They used it rarely. Even one Yadu death could bring a terrible punishment on a whole village. So it had to be targeted where the blow it struck could justify the deaths of innocent Xerappans which would follow.

'Who?' he said, surprised at the steadiness of his voice.

'Cozuman.'

Novan did start then. *The High Sorcerer!* He felt the stranger force him back into his seat.

'We have one chance. It may never happen again. I don't know if a mere leopard-driver can get that close. It may be necessary for you to use your sister.'

Grandmother Luella gave a stifled moan. She had never lived in the lost lands on the other side of the hills, like his father's parents. The man's voice went on unmoved. 'We thought of briefing her, along with you, but it seemed better to wait until she was asleep. She's young yet. She wouldn't willingly betray your secret, but she might not be able to hide her fear from the enemy. You have our permission to tell her only at the last moment, if it becomes necessary to use her.'

34

'Can either of us get close to Cozuman?' Novan almost spat the name. The High Sorcerer of the Children of Yadu. Supreme Commander of the Sorcerer Guard. The ruler of Mount Femarrat, whom everyone dreaded.

'He's closely guarded, of course. Cozuman is the most hated man in Yadu. Even his own people fear him, and every Xerappan loathes him. With good reason.'

'Sea Pines,' growled Novan's father.

A shudder of sorrow ran through the room at that name. It had not been enough for the Sorcerer Guard to drive them out of the coastal plain by magic or force. Cozuman had used other ways to make them go. On his orders, every man, woman and child in the village of Sea Pines had been slaughtered.

'Yes!' The stranger's confirmation was savage. 'That broke our resistance. Our people fled over the hills, and left the best land to them. Your parents, your grandparents, and you, a babe in arms. Oh, I know the Children of Yadu deny such a thing ever happened. They rely on Lord Cozuman too much to admit the truth, even to themselves. But we shall never forget.'

Grandfather Elyas and Grandmother Roann hissed their agreement. They seemed to have come to life in a way Novan had never seen before. He would be doing this for them, for all Xerappans.

'How can I get the poison to him? There'll be guards everywhere.'

'We've been watching you. You're an intelligent lad. And, more importantly, you have a jerboa with a reputation which outstrips all others.'

Novan started. Why hadn't Thoughtcatcher warned him of the stranger's presence? And where was the stranger's jerboa? He looked down. The other jerboa was big, like this rebel leader. Almost the size of a rat.

Thoughtcatcher was crouched beside the hearth, in the shadow of the log basket. Just two bright eyes, round and intelligent. Had Thoughtcatcher kept quiet because he wanted this to happen?

No thought came to him. There seemed to be a stillness and a darkness in his mind. It was as though even Thoughtcatcher had been silenced.

'The two of you will find your opportunity and seize it. For love of Xerappo.'

The big man released Novan and moved into the middle of the room. He leaned over the table and poured himself a beaker of milk. His left hand pulled the yellow scarf away from the lower part of his face. The lamplight was shaded, but enough of it escaped upwards to show a glimpse of a fleshy nose and jaw, a black moustache and a close-trimmed, curling beard. For a moment the beaker hid his face as he drank.

When he lowered it, he turned to face Novan. Milk beaded his moustache. His dark eyes found the boy's and held them. He smiled. Novan felt himself fall captive to those shining eyes. He knew this was an act of supreme trust. By showing his face, the stranger was putting his life in Novan's hands. He must prove himself worthy of such responsibility.

Almost before he could take in what had happened, the man drew his disguise around him again. A moment later, he was gone, shutting the door quietly as he stepped out into the darkness.

Novan sat shaken, acutely conscious of the little package that lay on the table just beyond his fingers. The others too, his parents, his grandparents, seemed paralysed.

'Do you know who that was?' said Grandfather Elyas hoarsely.

Novan shook his head.

'Big Knife.'

Novan had never heard that name before, and yet he felt he

should have. A racing part of his mind told him that these older members of his family must have known this man already, even seen his face. They must have told him about Novan, about Mina, about the journey into Yadu, about Thoughtcatcher.

Again he looked accusingly for the jerboa. The round black eyes shone knowingly from the hearth.

'She's very strong, his jerboa. You find yourself telling her more than you mean to.' The tone that entered Novan's mind was almost apologetic. Novan could not remember a time when Thoughtcatcher had not seemed in control. It was scary.

He was committed. Looking back, he could not quite remember the point at which he had crossed the divide, the moment when he could have said no, and did not.

Now the package of grommalan poison was his. Grandmother Roann would stitch it into the embroidered collar of his shirt. He would carry it into Yadu, to Mount Femarrat itself, into the headquarters of Lord Cozuman, whom they all hated. He would... But he could not imagine further than that.

He sat unmoving. He was being given this one chance to deliver his country. It was up to him. He could feel the older generations watching him.

Chapter Six

It is hard to be inconspicuous when you are holding a team of four leopards by the bridle. Yet Novan tried. The cold, bright security lighting of the Colony sent the remains of night scuttling outside the Fence. Novan stood caught in its beams, marked out as suspect by his Xerappan clothes, the coarse unbleached cloth of baggy trousers and loose shirt, with colourful embroidery at the neck and hems. The only disguise was servility: bowed head, downcast eyes, expressionless face. The fact that Xerappans tended to be shorter than the Children of Yadu helped.

His blood beat faster as a twittering swelled, which might have been the dawn chorus of birds, if it had not been so early. The door of the Yekhavu house was opening, spilling more light on the path. Alalia and her party were coming out.

Even if the lights had not been so bright he would have picked her out at once. She was the tallest of the women in her family. For this journey she wore a long, floating dress of blue-green, the colour you might see in a mountain torrent when the snow melts. Her long silver-blonde hair had been brushed straight and shining over her shoulders. Intricate silver jewellery twined around her throat and arms. Where it was exposed, her pale skin glistened, as it always did, with the creams the Yadu needed to protect them against the glare of the sun. There was an awning for the chariot Novan had made ready, but it would not be needed until day broke.

He scarcely looked at the smaller, stouter woman alongside her. Alalia's mother, Emania Yekhavu.

He drew his mind back from the vision of Alalia to the leopards. They stirred restively as the little crowd approached. He had to trust that Thoughtcatcher would be concentrating all his powers on stilling them. Yet as their groom, Novan must appear to be the one soothing and restraining them. The Yadu must not suspect anything else. He stroked the lead leopard's head and crooned in his ear.

Suddenly the cat bared his teeth. Novan had started. Among the chattering girls behind Alalia he had seen Mina... and almost not recognized her. She was dressed as he had never seen her before. Gone was the coarse but colourful gown, embroidered like his own shirt, in which she had walked up the hill to the Colony beside him. Now she was wearing the dress of a Child of Yadu, flimsy, expensive cloth that seemed to take wing as she walked. Dark red, setting off the lighter, shifting hues of Alalia's own. He felt a stab of fury, as though she had betrayed him. Mina tossed her black curls defiantly, seeming to know what he was feeling.

And then a lump of fear threatened to choke Novan. Where could Mina's jerboa be hiding? There was no longer that wide hem of embroidery, with its hidden pocket. Could Mina really be going into the heart of Femarrat, the centre of the Sorcerer Guard, without the protection of Whisper?

A tiny thought pierced his brain. '*Don't worry. You can't see Whisper, but she's here. She'll leap on board a baggage cart as soon as it's safe.*'

Then it was gone, like a light switching off. Thoughtcatcher had more than enough to do controlling the leopards.

All the same, Novan was uneasy. Big Knife had said he might need Mina's help to kill Cozuman. How could he be sure of communicating with her, if she and her jerboa were not always together?

39

There was a man's voice too, strong above the excited chatter of the girls. Alalia's father hugged his tall daughter. 'I wish I could be there for your betrothal ceremony. But there are too many rumours going round of a plot by the Xerappans. Nothing definite, but a feeling of something big going on. I need to be here at the Colony. Balgo will look after you and your mother. You'll be safer in Yadu than here. And a year from now, we'll have the biggest wedding for you this Colony has ever seen. So go to Femarrat and make your first vows to Digonez without me. Make sure that young man signs on the dotted line, so that you've got him where you want him.'

'I thought *he* wanted *me*!' Alalia's laugh came light and clear.

'It's a good match all round,' said her mother. 'You'll suit each other.'

'And one day,' said her father, 'a grandson of mine may be High Sorcerer on Mount Femarrat. Think of that.'

'Steady on,' laughed Alalia. 'I'm in no hurry to be *that* tied down!'

The farewells were over. Alalia and Emania, her mother, were in the chariot. For a moment Novan's hand had thrilled as he handed her up. She had hardly looked at him.

'I hope you know what you're doing with those brutes,' Emania Yekhavu said. 'Just remember, if they harm one hair of a Child of Yadu, it's your village will pay.'

Novan shuddered. That was the standard of Yadu justice under the Conquest. Twenty lives to pay the price of one. That was how little each Xerappan was worth. That was why they were helpless to free themselves.

The stiffly embroidered collar of his shirt rubbed against his skin as he turned away from Emania. Would he dare? Even if he got close enough to Lord Cozuman to administer the poison, could he really kill him? What price would his people

40

pay for *that*? It hardly bore thinking about. But High Sorcerer Cozuman was the heart of the evil which was crushing them. On his orders, hundreds of innocent people had been massacred and thousands driven from their homes. If Cozuman were gone, might it all be different?

As he mounted the charioteer's seat, Novan found himself looking directly into Alalia's face. He felt the prick of conscience. Why was it so difficult to see her as the enemy, even though she was the daughter of the Colony's governor?

She looked back at him, suddenly seeming to see him as a human being. First her lips, then her eyes, smiled at him. She was excited, happy. She wanted to share her mood with everyone. Grey-green eyes, clear, lively, looked into his. He felt the blood rush to his face, and was glad her brother Balgo was not near enough to see.

Mina and the other girls were climbing on board the larger carts pulled by lions. The baggage had been loaded already under canvas. Almost before he knew what he was doing, Novan had turned to face the road and was lightly touching the whip that sent the leopards smoothly forward.

They were nearing the Fence. Their armed escort, mounted on camels, stood ready. Six sorcerers, equipped with their spell-rods. Balgo was riding a white camel, his plum-red uniform perfectly washed and ironed. Waiting behind a captain, a sergeant and three experienced sorcerers, the young probationer looked shy and awkward. Novan felt a ridiculous surge of pride as he steered his chariot alongside them.

Captain Erekigan raised his arm. Words were being chanted. Dark dragons danced on the limits of Novan's vision. The Fence was parting. They were leaving the Colony's lights behind them. Before the day was over, they would leave Xerappo behind them. They would be in the land of Yadu.

At the foot of the hill they passed Novan and Mina's home, but

41

it was too dark to see anything. The house lay among trees some distance from the road down a smaller track. The lamp, which had been lit for Novan and Mina to get dressed by after their brief sleep, was out now. It was not wise for a Xerappan house to draw attention to itself. But Novan knew they would be gathered outside, his parents and grandparents. They would be listening for the rattle of wheels over stones, seeing their distant silhouettes against the starlight.

The scent of lemon trees hung in the air like a farewell gift.

Slowly, relentlessly, the sky lightened, banishing the stars. The convoy began to take on its true colours. Balgo, handsome in his red uniform, high on his white camel, looked more confident now. As the sun heaved up over the hills in a blaze of glory he pulled his cap lower to shade his eyes, put on his sunglasses, and settled the cloth that would protect the back of his neck.

With Thoughtcatcher's help, Novan stopped the chariot. He turned, keeping his face impassive. 'Shall I raise the awning?'

'Of course!' Emania snapped. 'Do you want us to be fried?' Already her face was pink and glistening, both with the sun-cream and with perspiration.

The canopy Novan pulled into position over his passengers was dark green cloth, deeper than the shifting turquoise of Alalia's dress. Long white fringes hung down, almost to the chariot's wooden sides. No sun would reach the women's arms, yet the light breeze of their passage could filter through and check the worst of the stifling heat. As he locked the struts into place, he was close enough to smell Alalia's perfume of roses. Would a young lady like her ever smell of sweat, as his mother and his sister did after a hard day's work?

She smiled at him again, slowly, tantalizingly. 'Thank you.' Her voice sank deeper than usual. It disconcerted him. Quickly he was back in his seat and coaxing the leopards on.

'*It's not natural,*' whispered Thoughtcatcher. '*Leopards should be sunning themselves on rocks or taking a nap up a tree. They weren't made to pull chariots, let alone work in the heat of the sun.*'

'Like jerboas?' Novan thought back to him, behind a smile.

The little desert rats were nocturnal. Thoughtcatcher was content to nestle in Novan's sleeve during the day. But when the shadows fell, he came alive, agile, athletic, on his thin springy back legs. Novan wondered where Whisper was in the convoy behind him. But he trusted her nimble intelligence. She would be hiding as near to Mina as she could safely get.

A thought blacked out his mind without warning. Mina, in her crimson dress like the Yadu. She had been made to leave her Xerappan clothes behind. What if that happened to Novan? If his concealing smock and trousers were taken away and he was forced into a new uniform? What would happen to the slender cylinder of grommalan stitched into the collar? He felt a cold sweat, even in the morning sun.

Down here in the valley the heat quickly grew intense. All around him were the high hills of Xerappo. But on every flattened peak stood a new Yadu colony. Novan had never felt so painfully how surrounded his people were, how intimidated, how hemmed in. This part of his country still had its old name, but for how much longer? How long before the Children of Yadu stopped the pretence that the coastal plain alone was theirs, and took over this hill country in name, as well as in reality? 'But it's our home!' the colonists would say, lifting innocent hands. 'Our children were born here.' Then the Xerappans would be left with no home at all.

He must not weaken. He must find a way to strike at Cozuman. He must end this.

'Captain!' called out Emania. 'This is intolerable. I'm jolted to death and ready to collapse with heat. Aren't we going to rest?'

Captain Erekigan urged his sand-gold camel closer to the chariot. 'Madam,' he said, 'we shall certainly rest for several hours around noon. But if we're to cross into Yadu today, we ought to press on for a while longer. However, if you like, we can pause for a short while for you to ease your legs. There's a stream here and some tamarisk trees to shade you. You girls,' he shouted to the cart behind the chariot, 'bring some fruit juice for your mistress.'

Novan, too, was glad of the break. He found himself stiffer than he had expected as he climbed down to hold the leopards. It must be the tension. He stroked the animals' hot, dense coats. Their gold and black blazed like this sandy desert country. The only green was the stripe of bushes and small, feathery trees that lined the stony stream bed. The girls were trailing towards it, bright and noisy as a flock of parakeets. Mina was among them. In spite of her red dress, you would not have mistaken her for a Child of Yadu, with her short stature and her black curls.

A cry of irritation rose from Alalia's mother. 'Call this a stream? There's hardly enough water to wash the dust from one's feet.'

To his consternation he heard Mina reply. 'No, ma'am. There used to be more, but the colonies have used the springs in the hills for their irrigation and swimming pools. This is all that's left for the valley.'

'Insolence! That girl's a Xerappan. What is she doing here? How dare you criticize Yadu policy?'

'Ma,' came Alalia's amused reply. 'You know perfectly well she's my maid, Mina. We discussed it. If I'm going to be betrothed to Lieutenant Digonez, I have to have a personal maid to keep up appearances. I'm not a schoolgirl now. *You've* got a Xerappan maid.'

'Pakann has more sense than to answer when she's not spoken to. That girl should be whipped.'

'For speaking the truth? You asked why this stream was so low. She told you.'

'As though it were a crime to grow fruit and to keep ourselves clean and refreshed. Of course we need that spring water.'

Mina bobbed a curtsy. Her face was very white. Novan almost groaned when he realized she still did not have the sense to keep quiet. 'I'm sorry, ma'am. I only meant that you can't use the water twice.'

'And you, I suppose, think the Xerappans should have priority?'

Mina was silent then.

'Well, it's too late to send her back,' Emania said at last. 'But watch her.'

She stalked away to settle herself under the flimsy shade of the tamarisks, slipping off her sandals and letting her hot, swollen feet cool in the shallow rivulet between the stones. The Yadu girls followed suit. Mina stood back, head bent.

Novan longed to walk across, scold her, comfort her. Anything to show solidarity. It was fantastically brave to speak out as she had done, but ridiculous too. And dangerous. Not only for her, but for their mission, to kill Cozuman. They mustn't draw any suspicion on themselves. He had had nearly two years working at the Colony. He had learned how to become almost invisible, recognized only for the service they wanted from him, his skill with the big cats. Mina must not endanger that. She lacked his experience. It would be best if nobody guessed he was her brother.

Their mission? But, of course, Mina hadn't been told. She had been up in the loft asleep when Big Knife had emerged from the shadows and the packet of poison had been laid on the table beside Novan's hand.

A tiny movement caught his eye. Something had hopped from the shelter of one bush to another, close to Mina's feet.

He saw her start and glance down, then her head shot up and she looked straight at him. He turned away, hoping desperately that no one else had seen.

'*She may learn something,*' Thoughtcatcher nudged him. '*If Whisper thinks she needs to.*'

'Big Knife said it was better if she didn't,' Novan's thought ground back. 'She might not be able to keep a secret. And I see what he meant.'

'*Jealous?*' observed Thoughtcatcher. '*You'd like to have answered Emania Yekhavu back like that, wouldn't you? Told her the truth about why the farmlands of Xerappo have run dry?*'

'What good will it do? It'll only get her into trouble, and then she's no use to us.'

'*So honesty must die, to serve your noble cause?*'

'That's what happens when you're conquered.'

'*Perhaps they haven't conquered Mina.*'

'Don't be daft.'

Oniron, the lion groom, was at his elbow. 'Lend me Thoughtcatcher, and I'll mind the leopards for a few minutes while you get a drink.' The more muscular lions had collapsed in the dust and one shaggy male had rolled over on his side with his eyes shut.

Novan grinned. 'Thanks. I'll be back in a flash.'

He had not realized how hot he was until he came under the shade of tamarisks and saw the water. He kept a polite distance from the women and was careful to move downstream, so that no one could complain he had fouled the stream for them.

As he crouched on a boulder and let a tiny waterfall fill his palms, a shadow fell across him. How did he know without turning that it was Alalia? He waited for her to speak. There was only silence.

He drank, shook the water from his hands, and stood up.

It was her. And this time it had not been Thoughtcatcher who had pushed that knowledge into his mind. He had felt her presence, as though she were more real than anyone else. She stood watching him, on the edge of the dappled shadows, with a half-smile which seemed oddly sad. Just behind her was a friend whose name Novan could not recall, watching them both with suppressed laughter.

The silence lengthened. Novan did not know whether it would be impolite to speak or to go.

Captain Erekigan delivered him. 'You, cat-drivers! Get these beasts on their feet. We need to be up in the hills for a midday camp long before noon.'

Suddenly everything was normal again. He was the servant charioteer, she was his passenger and employer, talking merrily to her mother about the dress and the jewellery she would wear for her betrothal ceremony.

'It's a pity your father can't be there,' said Emania. 'But Balgo will stand in for him.'

Alalia fell abruptly serious. 'Do you think there really is a danger? The Xerappans can't attack our Colony, can they?'

'They wouldn't dare. You just have to keep them in their place, that's all.'

Novan's hands closed tighter on the leopards' reins.

Emania settled back on the cushions. 'At least once we're in Yadu we shan't have to keep looking over our shoulders all the time. We'll be safe there.'

Chapter Seven

This valley in the ring of hills was not wide. Soon they were climbing the further slopes towards a cleft in the hilltop, where a bright blue arrow of sky pointed to the pass out of Xerappo. The sandy floor of the valley was giving way to boulders and gnarled bushes. Where the road ran up past a narrow terrace Captain Erekigan halted.

'Pitch the rest camp there.' He pointed with his camel whip. 'Where that overhang gives a bit of shade.'

Quickly the Xerappans set up the striped tents with their tasselled poles. The ground under the frowning brow of cliff was not only shaded, but even a little damp. On the canvas floor of the tents Mina and the other maids spread jewel-bright cushions.

As Novan handed Alalia down from the chariot he saw that, for all the cool colours of her dress, her face was flushed with heat. She staggered a little as her weight touched the ground. He held her firmly.

'Take your hands off my sister, beast-boy. She's not a lump of raw meat to be mauled by you.'

He had not seen Balgo behind him. Novan let go of Alalia immediately, overcome with fury and embarrassment.

Alalia turned a tired smile on her brother. 'I can defend my own honour, thank you. I nearly lost my balance. The leopard boy caught me.'

'I've seen him staring at you too many times. He should

keep his filthy eyes on his animals.'

'Balgo, it's too hot to argue. I'm going to lie down.'

She ducked under the tent flap into the restful shade.
Balgo looked down from his greater height on Novan. 'What
did she say to you by the stream?'

'Nothing.'

'I don't believe you.' There was a hostile pause. 'I'm
watching you.'

The Xerappan boy bowed his head. It was no good
answering back.

He unharnessed the leopards, keeping a single bridle on
their gold-studded collars. With Thoughtcatcher's help, he
led them into the shade. Their coats twitched at the touch of
the moist earth. They lapped at a puddle, where a spring
seeped through the rock, then stretched their languorous
bodies to sleep. Inside the tent, Alalia would be relaxing her
long limbs like that. Novan resolutely turned his thoughts
away.

Captain Erekigan was drawing a ring of defence round the
noon camp. The magic gave Novan a strange feeling. He knew
it was meant to keep dangers out. The wild boar that rooted
amongst the scrub on these hillsides? Xerappan
revolutionaries creeping up through the undergrowth? But
the Sorcerer Captain did not know that Novan was sitting
here inside his circle of defence with a packet of poison
hidden in his shirt collar.

Three sorcerers settled themselves around the
circumference of this invisible ring. One faced across the
hillside to the south, another to the north over the road, the
third west, back down into Xerappo. No one could attack
them from the east, where the cliff soared above the
overhang. The guards squatted, their rods resting
conspicuously on their knees. They kept them pointing
outwards, ready. Those white cylinders, capped with gold,

looked innocent enough. You would not think that from something so simple, almost beautiful, could flash instant death. Novan had to wrestle to break the fascination the spell-rods had over him. Balgo was already aware of how Novan felt in Alalia's presence. If he knew what else was occupying the leopard-driver's thoughts...

Like everyone else, except the three sentries, Novan lay down and tried to rest.

The sun was slipping lower in the sky, the heat more bearable, as they struggled to the top of the pass. The colony here was military, not agricultural. No orchards softened the slopes. All the natural vegetation had been hacked away. The cliff faces and the scree had been covered with metal nets, the slightest touch on which would sound alarm bells in the guard post. Across the V-shaped cleft that marked the summit of the road, a Fence bigger than the one around the Mount of Lemon Trees hung glittering against the sky. Though it was not solid, it confused the eyes, making it impossible to see beyond it.

Captain Erekigan's camel paced forward. The officer spoke authoritatively to the border guards, handed down papers. Impressive though the convoy of the wife and daughter of a colony's governor was, they were not automatically waved through. One by one they were subjected to individual scrutiny as the column edged slowly towards the border Fence. Emania and Alalia were given a respectful salute. Novan bowed his own head. He could feel the hostility and suspicion of the Yadu sorcerers inspecting him. What if one day the unthinkable happened, and a jerboa changed sides, so enabling the Yadu to read Xerappan thoughts?

He felt a blow like a whiplash in his mind. He had forgotten Thoughtcatcher's closeness.

'Sorry!' he whispered, before he could stop himself.

'What did you say?' a border guard challenged him.

'Nothing,' muttered Novan. 'Sorry.'

Surely they must have search-spells that would give him away? He felt their concentration, saw their rods, not ostentatiously waved, but questing, now this way, now that, probing him. They were not satisfied.

'Get down.'

Novan was trembling. They knew. 'What are they thinking?' his mind questioned Thoughtcatcher, but the jerboa was concentrating on holding the leopards.

The guards had abandoned their rods now. Their hands were searching Novan. As he stepped down from the chariot he had felt a wriggle at his trouser cuff as Thoughtcatcher slipped out just in time to escape detection. It was always like this, living on the edge, when one wrong movement, a delayed response, could mean it was all over. The sentries' hands were casually brutal, prodding, squeezing, with an occasional chuckle when he gasped with pain. They fingered his stiffly embroidered collar and passed on.

'Seems clean.'

'You never know, do you? They're tricky beggars.'

It was over. They hadn't said anything to release him, but their attention was moving on to the next cart. Oniron would soon be suffering the same treatment. Novan was free to climb back on to his seat.

What would happen when they got to Mina? He thought of their rough, searching hands and shivered.

It took a long time. The shadows were lengthening. A boy was sent out of the guard post carrying a tray of fruit juice for the passengers. No one offered a drink to Novan.

At last the convoy was cleared. The senior officer turned his rod to the Fence which filled the gap between the highest peaks. Two others, Novan noticed, aligned their rods with his. There must be a more powerful spell closing this frontier Fence. Again those words of power, which he could never

51

properly hear, still less remember. He shuddered nonetheless.

As the mesh began to gather in upon itself, the brightness grew more intense. It was hard to look at it, and yet Novan did not want to look at anything else. Great skirts of diamond-patterned metal concertinaed together, forming sparkling pillars either side of the road. All he could see through the gap was a column of sky, paler blue now, just beginning to be suffused with rose where the rays from the west caught the shifting motes of dust that hung thick in the air.

Thoughtcatcher moved the leopards before Novan had stirred from his trance to lift the reins or touch the whip. The camels were striding disdainfully past as the leopards strained to set the chariot rolling. Soon it would be over the crest and needing the brake.

Now he came level with the frontier Fence. He felt the tingle of its force down his spine. The Xerappans had nothing to combat this, only bare hands, flung stones, and, if they dared, poison. And only then if they were prepared for their own people to pay the price.

They were through. The curtains of metal were closing behind them. The frontier was sealed. And in front of him, like a dream come true, spread the eastern plain, densely green with orchards, sheltering little white villages, glittering with canals, all the way to the bright circumference of the sea.

He was back in his homeland. The last time he had been here he had been a tiny boy, a refugee, fleeing in his parents' arms.

And out of that plain, meeting his eyes with the shock of longing realized, rose an impossibly perfect white cone. It could only be Mount Femarrat. Perfect, except that the peak had been sliced away. In its place, like a giant spider, crouched a black temple.

Chapter Eight

He felt he was on holy ground. He wanted to jump down from the chariot, kneel on the earth of his homeland, seize handfuls of the soil and kiss it.

He could not, of course. He must still appear to be the mute, meek servant of the Yekhavu family. This was their land now. Yadu. Pain and anger knifed him.

'At last!' exclaimed Emania Yekhavu. 'Proper roads. We shan't be shaken about like peas in a drum now we're back in a civilized country.'

The road surface had changed abruptly as soon as they crossed the border. In conquered Xerappo, even the main roads were rough and stony. Here on the Yadu side of the border, the stones had been pulverized and compacted into a broad highway as unyielding as rock.

The chariot started to roll down the hill. Novan's eyes were intent now on what lay ahead. Lower and lower, out of the rocky hills, the road looped in horseshoe bends. The green of the plain was coming up to meet them like a flooding tide. Novan had seen fruit farms in Xerappo, irrigated with water diverted from the Xerappan streams. But here was the rich farmland his parents and grandparents had told him of. Mile after mile of orchards fruiting luxuriantly out of the black soil. Market gardens juicy with lettuces and cucumbers. Buffaloes with sleek, black hides. His grandparents Elyas and Roann had had such a farm as this, with orange trees and pineapples, before the Yadu sorcerers drove them out.

The day was declining and the shadow of the mountains was falling before them across the plain. That glimpse of the distant sea was narrowing and narrowing as they dropped lower, till it became a thin, bright fingernail and disappeared. Yet still Novan saw, far away across the levels, that single hill rearing like a volcano, just short of the coast. Even if he had not been brought up on tales of its magical history, he would only have had to look at Mount Femarrat, soaring dramatically out of the plain, to know this could be no ordinary hill.

'Pull up, curse you! Have you gone to sleep?' Novan was suddenly conscious of the angry captain shouting down at him from the saddle of his camel. He was aware belatedly that Thoughtcatcher too had been trying to attract his attention for several seconds. The jerboa had now stopped the leopards anyway, though Novan was still urging them on. That had been a dangerous carelessness.

'Sorry,' he muttered.

He had not even noticed the inn he had almost overshot. Certainly it was large enough to explain Captain Erekigan's indignation. If Novan had not been entranced by the spell of Mount Femarrat, he would have stared at it in amazement. He had never seen anything like it in Xerappo. Date palms, thicker and taller than he had known they could grow, clustered in a shady border around a square. The enclosure was formed by two-storey buildings, intensely white, with domed roofs. A wide gateway offered a welcome into a courtyard, where a fountain played.

Novan belatedly gave the appearance of reining in the leopards, and sat gazing in astonishment. It was several moments before he could explain to himself the cause of his surprise.

It was Alalia who realized, with a note of wonder in her voice. 'There's no Fence round it!'

This was clearly a Yadu hostelry, and bigger than any building on the Mount of Lemon Trees. Yet there was no sign of sorcerer sentries, with spell-rods always alert for danger. A middle-aged woman sat knitting in the evening shade beside the open gateway. She wore no red uniform. As the convoy halted, she wound up her ball of wool, spiked it on the needles, and got to her feet unhurriedly. Her smile was ready, as she lifted an untroubled face.

It was some satisfaction to Novan to see her eyes widen with shock as she took in the leopards and lions. She quickly recovered herself, but kept a wide distance as she skirted them to speak up to the captain.

'You'll be the betrothal party from the Mount of Lemon Trees. They told me you'd passed the frontier.'

So did they have thought-senders, after all? And over such a distance?

He followed her eyes back up to the distant peak. From the west, the sunset light warmed the Fence that filled the pass. He could see the guard post clearly. His anxiety lessened. Easy enough to signal down to this inn. Surely every traveller coming down off the hills would want to stop here for refreshment? She was not a guard, though she might still be a sorcerer. She would know everything that passed on this road.

He and Thoughtcatcher steered the leopards in under the arch to the paved courtyard. Beyond, through another archway, there was a stable yard, but the passengers would alight here by the fountain. The music of its water was itself refreshing.

He watched with a pang of loss as all the Children of Yadu descended from chariots and carts and swept in a coloured flock into the inn's cool interior. Alalia was gone, until tomorrow, and without a look at him. He and Oniron and the other Xerappan drivers must take their beasts and vehicles on into the further yard.

It was bigger, barer, more exposed. The floor was sand, not cool paving stones. No fountain splashed; there was just a pump for watering the animals. A dozen camels already squatted in the open, as if they owned the space. In the open stables around, shadows moved. As he halted the leopards and began to unhitch the empty chariot, Novan peered closer. There were beasts tethered in the stalls which he had never seen before. Much smaller than camels, with long ears and sweet faces – sweeter than the harsh bray which broke from one of them.

'*Donkeys!*' Novan called to Oniron in excitement. 'My grandfather told me about them. But I've never seen one till now.'

'Here? We're hardly over the mountain! Can it be this different here from home already?' Then, as the excitement caught him too, 'Do you think there'll be horses?'

'Bound to be. But did you see the inn-woman's face when she saw our leopards and lions?'

Oniron rocked with laughter. 'She was trying not to show she was scared, but her eyes were popping out of her head!'

'That's why Alalia wanted to bring them.' Novan started to rub the dust and sweat from his charges' coats. 'To impress the Children of Yadu this side of the border. The Yekhavus don't want Cozuman's family to think they're some rustic yokels from the backwoods. The colonists have got a style of their own.'

'You sound almost proud of it. As if you were one of them.'

'I'm not! How dare you?'

'Keep your voice down. We're being watched.'

Their six guards, even Captain Erekigan, had led their own camels into the stable yard and tethered them. They were overseeing their feeding and watering, sending the inn's ostlers running. Most of the servants here, Novan noticed, were Xerappans, judging from their dark hair and shorter stature. The officers were sauntering away now, back to the guests' courtyard, from where the distant talk and laughter of the women floated through the archway. One of the six sorcerers detached himself from the group and came across to the boys with a more purposeful stride. It was Balgo.

'We've hired stalls for the cats. Tether them, and make sure the doors are firmly bolted, top and bottom. To make doubly sure, you'll sleep in the stalls with them tonight.'

All the Xerappan boys started violently, as if his spell-rod had struck them. At the cuff of his trouser leg, Novan felt Thoughtcatcher wince.

'But we can't...' Novan started to protest. 'Not while we're asleep.'

'They'll eat us,' said Oniron.

Thoughtcatcher and the other jerboas had applied their concentration at full stretch all day. They had made the unwilling cats drag their loads to the top of the pass, and held them under control on the steep descent. The little desert rats must be exhausted now. They could not stay awake all night.

Balgo's face registered a jolt of surprise, quickly brought under control. 'I thought you could make those big cats do anything you wanted.'

'Not in our sleep.'

'Well... all right. I suppose you could have the stall next door. Plenty of straw. I'll have food sent to you. But there must be no accidents. You must take it in turns to sit up and watch the brutes.'

He settled himself under the shade of a plane tree and beckoned to a serving-boy.

'He wants us to watch the cats, but he's going to watch us,' murmured Oniron. 'They don't trust us.'

They're right not to, Novan longed to tell him, but he kept silent.

Balgo leaned back against the treetrunk. He watched as the leopards and lions, growling surlily, were shut away for the night. The boy brought him wine and a plate of steaming couscous.

In the smaller courtyard, the rest of the Yadu party would be gathering for supper. Then they would retire to the upper rooms, behind balconies already deeply shadowed. Those rooms presented a blank back wall to the stable yard. It shut out the Xerappans, except Mina and Pakann, Emania Yekhavu's maid. Novan looked at the barrier separating him from the guests' courtyard. This was how it was going to be. He on the outside, Mina on the inside. He, guarded and watched with suspicion. She, trusted and free. He longed to finger the little package in the collar of his shirt, but stopped himself in time. Was it going to be possible to do what he had to, without Mina?

Where was Whisper? He tried to imagine what would happen if somebody spotted a little desert rat hopping across the clean, swept floors of this inn.

'She's under the bed,' came the reassuring answer.

'How far can your mind reach?' Novan's question was unspoken.

'Luckily Mina's room backs on to this yard. But I'm dead tired now. Just make sure those leopards are fastened up till tomorrow, will you? It's going to be a testing day.'

'Why?' But the question remained unanswered.

When the animals had been fed raw meat and bones, there was food for the Xerappans too. A tray of grain and vegetables, even a little meat, not very different from Balgo's meal, though with water only to drink. Balgo had finished eating. He clasped his hands behind his head, as he leaned back on the cushions the boy had brought him.

'This is the life, eh? If it wasn't for curs like you, I could be through there in that courtyard with my mates and the girls.

If I felt like it, I could walk out of the gate and take a stroll. No sentries, no Fence. The Children of Yadu can go anywhere they like without having to look over their shoulder all day. There isn't a Xerappan this side of the border would dare step out of line.'

The Xerappan drivers paused in their eating. No one spoke.

'Just you watch and learn. Don't tell me none of you here hasn't thrown a stone at the Yadu. I know your sort. But you're going to find out what it's really like in Yadu proper. We're in charge. This is our land. Just get that into your stubborn heads. And before long, the other side of those hills...' he nodded back towards Xerappo, '... is going to be all ours too. Not just colonies. It'll all be the land of Yadu, twice as big as it is now. Nobody can stop us.'

'You're prisoners though, aren't you?' cried out Linkat, the smallest Xerappan boy, suddenly daring. 'Like you said, back there you've got to have Fences, and guards everywhere you go. You're not free, any more than we are.'

Balgo rose, quivering with rage. He strode across and slapped Linkat's face, so that the boy fell sprawling on the sand, his supper spilled.

'*You're* the slaves; we're the masters. Get that?'

He flung himself back on the cushions under the tree, no longer relaxed and smiling. His fingers toyed with his spell-rod.

Novan sat raging. He and the others had not dared to lift a hand or raise a voice to defend Linkat. He hated himself for that.

Chapter Nine

He hated himself still more the next morning.

The party slept later than the day before and the Children of Yadu breakfasted around the fountain in the courtyard. Sometime in the night Balgo had been relieved. An older guard sat yawning under the plane tree as the light began to intensify towards sunrise. When the convoy took to the road the date palms were casting the first long shadows back towards the mountains. The hard-surfaced road glinted in the sun.

'Isn't it wonderful to feel the sea-breeze?' Alalia threw back the sleeves of her light dress. Novan tried to decide whether it was the same one she had worn yesterday. That coolly shifting play of blue and green, yet wasn't there today a hint of rose in the weave, bringing out the bloom of her cheeks? She looked even more wonderful.

He tried to concentrate on the leopards. He could not leave everything to Thoughtcatcher. In spite of himself, with every mile they travelled he felt his pride grow as lead driver of the convoy. They travelled along a road deeply shaded by trees, between whose trunks struck blinding bars of sunlight. At every whitewashed village the Children of Yadu ran out to stare at them. Clearly they did not use leopards for this on the plain. The cats themselves seemed to be enjoying the shade, prowling along the highway as though the chariot were no weight to them. Without the desert around them, their gold shone richer, pebbled with black. Novan sat up straighter, feeling himself for the first time in his life the object of awe and envy. There were tall Yadu boys with fair hair who would clearly have loved to sit where he was, in the charioteer's seat, holding the leopards' reins. And behind him, in the passenger seat, was the most beautiful of Yadu girls.

'Look, Ma!' Alalia giggled. 'Look at their faces. I knew we'd make a stir.'

If he turned, he would see the lions, pulling the heavier carts. They were big, broad-pawed, the males with richly tumbling brown manes. Only Xerappans could tame them.

And then the pride tasted bitter in his mouth because, after all, he was no better than a slave. He was as much under the power of the Yadu as the big cats were under the will of the jerboas. He was not here to enhance his own status, but the Yekhavu family's.

He studied the farms and villages as they passed, scanned the level fields beyond the trees. The Yadu here moved about freely, relaxed, not looking over their shoulders. There were no sorcerers guarding them, with white spell-rods conspicuously ready. It took him a little while to realize what else was strange. Almost everybody crowding to watch the convoy had fair hair. There was hardly a Xerappan in sight. Here, in what had once been half of Xerappo, people like him had almost vanished. Now and then he glimpsed gangs of labourers, harvesting fruit or vegetables in the fields, bending to the back-breaking work of picking strawberries or pulling radishes in the sun.

But mostly it was only the fair-haired Yadu around him. Confident, happy, in full possession of this land.

His land. Before the war.

At the heart of this Plain of Xerappo rose Mount Femarrat. Novan's heart lurched as he realized he was looking straight at it now, down the long avenue of jacaranda trees that were

61

scattering lilac-coloured petals all along the way. The solitary mountain was a cone so sheer it seemed it could not be an accident of nature. Had human hands raised it – or some power more than human?

'Femarrat!' He heard Alalia's low, thrilling cry, as if his own heart had spoken.

It was hard to think of anything else now, watching it grow slowly, oh so slowly, as the long level road crept nearer. The leopards' paws made no sound, the chariot creaked lightly over the smooth surface. There was the occasional harsh grunt or the rasp of a camel's hooves as one of the escort drew alongside for a while.

'Shall I raise the awning?' Novan turned to ask in an oddly hushed voice. He had not slowed the leopards.

'No!' Alalia cried at once. 'I want to see.'

'There's plenty of shade here,' her mother agreed. 'The roads in Yadu are properly planned. Not those baking tracks we have to put up with in Xerappo, with hardly a tree in sight.'

You felled our trees, Novan wanted to shout at her, so that we couldn't hide in them and throw stones at you.

His joy and pride were slipping away from him. His face no longer lit up as they entered another little town and the Yadu ran out to see the outlandish procession. But when they were past the houses he forgot it at once. Mount Femarrat had grown taller.

The pace was increasing. It was as though Femarrat were sending out a spell that pulled them ever more strongly as they drew closer. At first it had shimmered white against the blue sky and the deep-green avenue of trees. Now they could see that its bare slopes were streaked with purple and pale green. And there was that black building, where the summit should have been. Captain Erekigan's camel was stretching its neck forward, lengthening its stride. The chariots and carts were bowling along, their occupants hardly aware of the donkey carts passing them in the opposite direction. Taller animals trotted by, manes rippling. They had gone before Novan came to with a start.

'Horses? Were those *horses*?'

'*I thought you were never going to notice,*' Thoughtcatcher twitched.

Novan risked a glance over his shoulder. Now that he looked properly, he could see that the riders wore the red uniform of the Sorcerer Guard.

'*That's right. You're really going to need to be more careful,*' his jerboa observed.

The shade under the trees seemed colder for a moment. The breeze from the sea blew stronger. He had to tilt his head back now to see the top of Mount Femarrat. They were coming under its shadow. It was filling his vision, overawing him.

Suddenly the road swung right in a sweeping curve. All day it had been driving them straight towards Femarrat, as though there were nowhere else it could possibly go. Now the broad highway curved and there, round the shoulder of the mountain, they saw the glittering sea.

'Halt!' called Erekigan, as Novan, mesmerized, would have driven on round this bend.

A narrower fork continued the same inexorable line straight for the mountain. As though, thought Novan, it would penetrate right through into the heart of it. A small grey building stood at the junction. Half a dozen guards in red tunics stood or sat in the shade of its walls. They were not over-tense, but alert.

Captain Erekigan dismounted from his camel. This was a mark of respect he had not shown the guards at the border post. He raised his hand to touch his forehead in a salute and

63

handed over the convoy's papers. While these were being examined, two sorcerers came sauntering up. One crossed to the other side of the road and the pair moved slowly down the column. Their white rods angled inwards towards the strangers, scanning them one by one.

Novan, like all Xerappans, could never conquer the tension of such a search, the sense of guilt it caused, the fear of what the sorcerers might find. Until now he had been innocent, yet still felt afraid under their scrutiny. Now he was carrying death into the heart of their headquarters. Surely they must discover that?

He did not have long to wait. He was one of the first to go through the check. It seemed to take an age, although the sorcerers were walking slowly on all the time, one on either side of him. There was no flash from their rods. They passed to Alalia and Emania. He seemed to have forgotten how to breathe.

'This isn't the last search,' Thoughtcatcher warned him. *'Lord Cozuman is very thorough.'*

Even the Yadu from the Mount of Lemon Trees seemed subdued. Alalia Yekhavu might be the daughter of a colony governor, on her way to be betrothed to a rising star of the Sorcerer Guard, of Cozuman's family, but there would be no relaxation of security for her. Unsuspicious and peaceful the rest of Yadu might be, but Mount Femarrat stood apart from normal life. This was the nerve centre of sorcery, the furnace of power. Whoever held Femarrat held this land.

'Go safely, and good luck for your betrothal.' The guards were smiling now.

'He's a lucky fellow, that Digonez!' shouted one of them.

As though it had been nothing, just a formality. But Novan knew the check had been deadly serious.

He was past it. He was through. The leopards paced on as if in a dream.

'Stop the chariot!' Alalia cried out.

Novan obeyed, with Thoughtcatcher calming the surprised leopards. They were halfway between the guard post and the foot of the sacred mountain. There were no trees here. The sinuous bend of green continued around the curve in the main highway, towards the sea. This narrower road was bare. Security, Novan thought. No hiding place around Mount Femarrat. The atmosphere had become more like Xerappo than the rest of Yadu.

Captain Erekigan turned his camel and rode back to them. 'What's the matter, ma'am? Is anything wrong?'

'Call my maid.' Alalia sounded distressed. 'I need to make myself ready before we get there. I don't want Digonez to see me all in a mess after a day's travelling.'

'You should have thought of that at the guard post,' her mother said. 'They'd have let you borrow their bathroom, to change your dress and do your hair.'

'I couldn't! Didn't you see the way they were grinning at me, once they'd finished the search?'

'Sorcerers!' Emania shrugged. 'They think they're a cut above everyone else. No respect. Even Balgo's starting to get haughty with me.'

Erekigan beckoned. Mina scrambled down from the lion cart and came running.

'Do what you can,' said Alalia, 'there's a dear. Digonez hasn't seen me for nearly two years. I couldn't bear it if he looked at me and his face fell.'

You're lovely, Novan wanted to shout. If he doesn't realize he's the luckiest man in the world, he's an idiot.

Of course he said nothing. He was only her driver. He sat there while his sister busied herself brushing the dust from Alalia's pale hair till it shone, refreshing the rose perfume. A wave of it drifted over Novan, reminding him of the hint of rose colour in her iridescent dress. Her eyes were freshly painted, her hands creamed. All the time Emania kept up a stream of instructions to Mina.

'Whisper?' thought Novan.

'*She's there,*' Thoughtcatcher reassured him. '*In the shadow of the wheel.*'

It was risky, the little rodent on the smooth surface of the road, with no shelter but the chariot itself. Thoughtcatcher did not tell him what was passing between the two jerboas. Novan longed to talk to Mina, to make some plans. What if the arrangements were like their overnight stay at the inn, with Novan shut outside and only Mina and Emania's maid allowed amongst the Yadu? How late could he leave it before he told her what they had to do?

The urge to finger the poison in his collar was almost overwhelming.

At last it was over.

'Bring her a mirror,' Emania ordered.

Alalia studied herself. 'I suppose that will have to do ... Thank you, Mina.'

Novan's heart knew a rush of warmth. It was so rare, that word of thanks from the Yadu to the Xerappans for any services they rendered. Alalia was special, just as he'd always thought. She was different from the rest.

The convoy rolled on. Now Novan could see what was waiting for them at the end of this road. The towns and villages of Yadu might need no protection, but Femarrat was the exception. Around the base of the sacred mountain ran a Fence mightier than anything Novan had seen before. It did not have the ethereal shimmer of the one on the Mount of Lemon Trees or the border pass. It was massive, its lattice of metal slats broader than his hand, locked into a diamond-patterned trellis. Though silvered, it looked duller, greyer, more forbidding.

He felt a surge of anger. Femarrat was supposed to be

exquisitely beautiful, a fairy mountain you longed to go to and never wanted to leave. That was how the Xerappan legends described it. The Yadu sorcerers had made it ugly, repelling outsiders. Red uniforms clustered thickly where the Fence barred the road. It was impossible to count them distinctly through the mesh.

It was hard to make himself drive right up to it, hard to steady his breathing. He dared not look at the faces of the waiting sorcerers. He was glad that it was usual for a Xerappan to bow his head. A part of his soul still longed to look up, to see above and beyond the new Fence the fabled mountain, the old heart of Xerappo. But for now only one thing mattered: getting through that Fence without catastrophe.

If he had thought it would be a repeat of the rod-search at the road junction, he was wrong. Novan did not quite see how it happened, but suddenly he was aware that there were about twenty sorcerers outside the Fence, surrounding them. A red mist danced before his eyes, long after its particles had reassembled into human shapes. He could hear nothing, not even the whisper of Thoughtcatcher's mind. Dimly he knew he must have heard words of power which had blotted out all other words, and finally themselves.

'... password?' Abruptly, voices began again. Novan shook his head and blinked.

Erekigan looked nervous as he answered a senior sorcerer. Though Mount Femarrat must have been advised long since of the coming of the Yekhavus, their escort was grilled as though the guards had no knowledge of them.

This search left nothing to chance. Everyone, Yadu or Xerappan, was made to dismount and line up in front of the Fence. Novan could feel, with terror, the force close to his back. Even the Yekhavus looked pale.

First the white rods were trained over them, from head to

67

toe. One sorcerer was assigned to each traveller. Novan's was a middle-aged Sergeant Sorcerer, reflecting, Novan thought shrewdly, the level of suspicion towards him. Even Balgo, he noticed with astonishment, was being searched, though by a sorcerer not much older than himself.

Then came the physical search. Practised hands questing in every possible hiding place for a weapon. Novan almost choked when the sergeant's fingers squeezed the embroidered collar. But Grandmother Roann had done her work well. Between the stiff braid and coarse threads, the yielding cylinder of grommalan did not give its secret away. There had been nothing for the sorcerer's rod to respond to. Poison was the one weapon the Yadu had no means to counter. Their only shield was the massive revenge which would follow if it were used. Would even Cozuman's death be worth that?

'You Xerappans sweat like pigs.' The sergeant wiped disgusted hands on his red tunic.

Novan was shaking. He could not help it. 'Sorry,' he muttered. 'It's hot.'

The chariot and carts were being searched, everything emptied out on to the short grass and examined inside and out. Where was Thoughtcatcher, where was Whisper? He could feel no answering call. Had they hopped away unseen, to escape the search? Could they get back before the Fence closed behind the convoy?

They were boarding their vehicles again. Emania and Alalia looked shaken. 'The indignity!' Mrs Yekhavu said. 'As if we were no better than Xerappans.'

The Fence was opening. Though no flashes shot from it, its movement was like blinding light. You had to shut your eyes. You could not watch. You could not listen. You must not see or hear how it happened.

As the force struck them, the leopards gave a leaping howl.

This barrier was like nothing they had ever experienced. Novan hauled on the reins, desperately afraid they would bolt. Instead, they collapsed, pressed to the ground. Was it the power of this Fence alone that was subduing them? Was Thoughtcatcher back? Novan realized with huge relief that he must be. The trembling cats crouched low on their bellies, then, still quivering, slowly began to inch the chariot forward. Even with the Fence opened to the width of the road, it was like struggling against a gale. Nothing in human or beast wanted to cross that gap in the barrier, yet it seemed as though they must. As if in a nightmare, when you long to scream and run, yet cannot move, the legs of the cats and the camels, the wheels of the vehicles, dragged them, with enormous difficulty, across that short, crucial threshold.

Suddenly they were through, and released. The Fence was closing behind them. The sorcerers were grinning.

A welcome party stood watching their arrival.

'That's Digonez!' Novan heard Alalia's horrified cry. 'He's been watching the whole thing. The beast!'

'Alalia!' her mother gasped. 'He'll hear you! For goodness' sake remember where you are.'

'I'm not going to be allowed to forget it, am I, judging by that body search?'

When Novan looked round, her cheeks were flaming.

Only a few of the reception party were wearing the red uniform. There were women in gowns more elegantly styled than Emania's and Alalia's, men in loose, flowing robes. Yet all wore white headdresses, bound with a crimson cord. The eyes of many of them were hidden behind sunglasses.

A uniformed sorcerer stepped forward with a broad smile. He was much taller than Novan, and infuriatingly handsome, with fair, clipped hair. He held out both hands, courteous, as though the humiliating frisking of his guests had never happened.

'Emania Yekhavu, and Alalia. Welcome to Femarrat!'

'Lieutenant Digonez.' With a gracious smile, Emania let the young sorcerer lift her down.

Digonez came round to the other side of the chariot, though he paused to eye the leopards with searching curiosity. Again, those lifted arms, that ready smile.

'You look ravishing. How do you manage it, my sweet, after two days travelling on the open road?'

Novan could not hear what Alalia murmured as she let herself step down into his arms. When the pair walked past him, Digonez was still grasping her hand.

'I'll take you to your quarters. And then I have to show you off to my uncle Cozuman.'

Something of the same shiver went through Novan as he had felt when he stood with his back to the Fence. The High Sorcerer of Mount Femarrat. He was very close now.

Chapter Ten

It was like the inn again. Novan was separated from Alalia. Mina and Pakann, Emania's maid, followed the Yekhavu women and their Yadu hosts towards the dwellings that clustered on the lowest slopes of the hill. Linkat and Oniron led the slow-pacing lions behind them to deliver the luggage. Only Novan was left, with his leopards and the empty chariot. He tidied the cushions. They gave off a breath of Alalia's perfume. He thumped them in frustration.

A woman in the red uniform of a sorcerer was watching him through her sunglasses with amusement. 'You should think yourself lucky we've allowed you this side of our Fence. It's a privilege few Xerappans can boast of. You'll be able to go back to your hills and tell your grandchildren one day, "I stood on Femarrat".'

It did not help that this unknown woman was right. He was inside the Fence. All along he had feared that he might never be allowed on Mount Femarrat, that he would have to stable the leopards somewhere short of the holy mountain and wait helplessly for Alalia to return from her betrothal ceremony. But he was here. He had passed the most formidable barrier – probably.

'What shall I do with the leopards, ma'am?' Speak humbly. Disguise his anger that once every Xerappan in the country could gather here for the great festivals, when all this country was theirs.

'Follow me... These leopards are under control, aren't they?'

Are you afraid of them? he longed to say. Hide that grin, this one little triumph of superiority.

'It would be a pity to kill such remarkable brutes.' She flicked her rod casually.

Triumph disintegrated. Yadu sorcerers rarely took half measures with Xerappans. Their spell-rods could stun, but more often they killed. The sorcerers took no chances. At best, Novan thought, she might kill him at the first sign of danger and only stun the leopards.

She led him over black cobbles between low white houses. It would have been beautiful, if it had not been for the absence of greenery. Occasionally an upright cactus stood sentinel at a gateway or a window sill was made brilliant with geraniums, but there was little else to relieve the glare and the bright, bare lines of the buildings. This was not an agricultural colony, like the Mount of Lemon Trees, not a market town of the Yadu plain. It was a military headquarters, a stronghold of sorcery. Security came first.

Novan glanced up at the slopes of the mountain. Had there once been woods there? Yes, he remembered the story of his grandparents' wedding, the trees by the pool. Even as he thought of them, he gasped at the beauty still here. It was so much more complex and colourful than he had expected. The mount was not the perfect geometric cone it had appeared from a distance. There were clefts riven deep into the sides of the chalk-white hill, shadowed with purple. And winding down from the summit what seemed to be the icy green of a glacier. No. As he looked closer at its lower, gleaming falls, he saw that they were shaped into broad steps, their lips rounded, smoothly translucent as glass. A stairway to heaven? His heart ached at the thought.

Thoughtcatcher pulled his attention back. The sorcerer

had turned into a narrower alley, leading straight towards the hillside. Under a canopy of white rock, black holes gaped.

'Caves,' said the sorcerer. 'They're cool for stabling. We normally keep horses here, but I've moved them out. The smell of your big cats would terrify them.'

Novan hesitated. The semicircular arches of the cave mouths were open. There seemed to be no doors, no cage bars.

The woman had an uncanny knack of reading his feelings. She laughed. 'Put them in. There's water there already and you can bring food later. Don't look so puzzled. The Sorcerer Guard has more effective barriers than timber or steel.'

Novan obeyed. He settled the cats as well as he could, noting the deep, fresh straw in the shadowed interior, the water trough.

As he stepped out, he was still wondering what would keep these wild animals safe. The sorcerer clicked her fingers and drew them sideways. A thread of silvery wire followed her movements, spinning across the gap from a rock on one side to a wall on the other. One slender filament of light.

She smiled with satisfaction. 'Go on. Try it.'

Novan approached it. The force thrilled through his body, at the level of his stomach. At first it was almost pleasant, the next moment he felt sick. He jerked back.

'You see? It will not do the slightest harm to your beautiful leopards. But they won't want to pass it and nor will anyone interfering from outside. Theoretically, they could creep under it, but somehow, I don't think they will.'

It was their superiority, their utter confidence in themselves, that infuriated Novan. She was right, of course. The sorcerers' power was absolute.

'Where do I sleep?' His voice sounded surly, even to himself.

'Down there.' She had suddenly lost interest in him, now

the leopards were housed. 'The last house in the row is for you and the other drivers. Some of your sorcerer escort will be sleeping next door. We've made them responsible for your conduct. And of course, we have our own defences.' The smile returned, less pleasant this time.

She left him alone, as though he was free to go anywhere on Mount Femarrat. Yet he knew he was not.

He stood wondering. His own small bag was in the luggage cart Linkat was driving. His hands felt oddly empty. Should he go to the house and wait for the others? Explore, and find the limits of his liberty? Though he could see no guards, he was sure he was being watched.

Before he had decided, there was a clatter of wheels on the black cobbles. The lion carts were coming back. The young Xerappans driving them looked more light-hearted without their Yadu employers. Emania and Alalia's luggage had gone. There were only the small bundles of the Xerappan servants and the larger packs of their sorcerer escort. The tall camels, Novan realized, must have been given bedding somewhere else.

He waited while more Femarrat sorcerers oversaw the housing of the lions in the neighbouring caves, the storing of the emptied carts, the drawing of another Fence-wire. Now at last the boys came rushing towards him.

'What a place, eh?'

'Makes your eyes hurt, doesn't it? All this white.'

'You should see where they've gone. They've got a swimming pool and everything!'

'Yeah, and they don't have trees outside their houses, but they grow them *inside*.'

'There's courtyards, see, like at the inn, with pools and green stuff, like a proper garden.'

'Reckon they think they're finally safe when they get indoors.'

74

'Not like here.' Linkat looked round in wonder at the bare mountain. 'Even inside that blessed great Fence, they still think we'll get them.'

No one said anything for a while.

'That Cozuman,' Novan asked at last, his mouth dry. 'Did you see him?'

'No.' Oniron jerked his head over his right shoulder. 'By all accounts he lives up there. The Yekhavus are going there next. But not us.'

Novan squinted into the sun. Against the blinding white of the further slopes he could just make out a large white building. From within its walls a single tall cypress rose, like an almost-black spear. One of those winding glass-green staircases climbed to the house.

So far away. So bare and visible the approach. Even as he watched he could see a colourful knot of people climbing those steps. The crimson red of the Sorcerer Guard was prominent among them. Digonez would be there. He wondered what colour dress Alalia was wearing now.

He doubted that even Mina would be taken to the High Sorcerer's house. What hope had a Xerappan chariot driver of getting anywhere near it?

As evening fell, clouds of seabirds rose into the sky from the unseen ocean. Their cries rang in Novan's heart, wild, free. If only he were not on the landward side of Mount Femarrat. If only he could climb higher, work his way around the slope, he would see the waves running inshore, which until now he had only glimpsed as a distant brightness. What did those bird cries mean? Fishing boats coming home? From the quarters where the Yekhavu family had been taken, and still more from Cozuman's house high on its green staircase, you would be able to look out over the sea.

He and the other cat-drivers went to the back door of the

barrack kitchen, as they had been told. They collected raw entrails and gristle and bloody bones from the cooks.

'What kind of draught animal needs meat? We don't give this stuff to horses and camels. They must have peculiar habits in Xerappo.'

The boys hung their heads. A lifetime's training had taught them not to answer back.

'Lost your tongues? You do speak Yaduan, don't you?'

Novan answered for them, carefully. 'The colonists used to hunt the big cats for sport. Then they discovered that we could control them. So the Yekhavus thought it would be great to have their chariot pulled by leopards. Something nobody in Yadu would have.'

'Certainly bizarre. Though whether anyone in Yadu wants to be that outlandish is another matter.'

'Especially if it means you have to take a bunch of Xerappans everywhere with you.'

'I'm surprised they let them into Femarrat, myself.'

The cooks lounged in the doorway, talking to each other as though the Xerappans were not standing listening. Suddenly one said, 'Well, take your offal away, can't you? We've a hundred guards to feed in half an hour.'

The boys took their bloody loads back to the caves. A different sorcerer was waiting, not the one who had spun the Fence-wire for Novan's leopards.

'Throw it over.'

The wire was slender, almost invisible in the twilight. None of them wanted to approach it. Though it did not move, it thrummed with power. Novan had to force his limbs towards it. It was an effort to convince himself that it would not harm him, unless he touched it. Already he was beginning to feel that sickness knotting his stomach. When he could bear to go no closer he raised his arms and heaved the meat and bones towards the cave.

The leopards growled. From out of the shadows they started to emerge into the fading light. Their golden coats seemed to bring the sunlight back. Two of them leaped on the same knucklebone and snarled as they tried to wrench it from each other.

'Splendid! I back the taller one with the rings round its eyes.'

Novan spun round. He had been so taken up with his fear of the wire and his concern for the leopards that he had totally failed to notice the people coming up behind him. Digonez and – how could he have failed to be warned? – Alalia, with Balgo and half a dozen others. Even Mina inconspicuously in the rear.

'Thoughtcatcher?'

'Surprise, surprise! Well, I was trying to stop the leopards murdering each other. This Fence-wire keeps getting in my way.' Yet Novan thought he detected a quiver of laughter.

'Lieutenant Digonez is interested in your leopards.' Balgo sounded as though he felt awkward speaking to a Xerappan in the presence of an officer of Cozuman's élite Guard.

'Our leopards,' said Alalia, smiling straight into Novan's eyes.

'How do you control them?' There was no smile in Digonez's expression, yet he looked at Novan just as hard.

'Just by thinking,' Novan murmured, 'sir.' He remembered belatedly to hang his head, not to look either of them in the face. Yet his heart was singing from Alalia's unexpected smile.

'Show me.'

Novan jerked his eyes up then. Digonez had not relaxed his stare. 'Get into that pen and show me how you do it. Separate those two leopards from that bone.'

The sweat broke out on Novan. It was one thing to take sleek, well-fed leopards and harness them to the chariot. They might dislike it intensely, but they were familiar with the routine, and the girths and reins added a physical check to Thoughtcatcher's mind control. But to go into a pen where hungry cats were fighting over food...

'*Don't worry. Whisper's here. She'll help us.*' Thoughtcatcher's assertion came quickly, but Novan could sense the jerboa was frightened too.

'Shall I tell him it's better not to?'

'*Risky. I don't think Lieutenant Digonez is used to being argued with, let alone by a Xerappan.*'

'How do I get past the wire, sir?' Novan said, playing for time.

'You don't suppose I'm going to take it down for you, do you? And risk them attacking Alalia? You can get under that wire if you really try. I'll slacken the spell just a bit.'

Novan turned to face it, with the gorge rising in his throat. Could he do it? Could he lie on his stomach and wriggle his way under that sickening force? And what would that do to Thoughtcatcher? Could the jerboa still keep the leopards under control while the force battered his brain?

'*Should we just try doing it from here?*' the jerboa suggested.

Even as he whispered, the tallest leopard, Quercus, raised his head. The other snatched the bone away. At once the first leopard leaped upon it, teeth piercing the smaller cat's jaw. Novan cried out in dismay.

'*The wire's interfering. I can't hold them.*'

Novan was down on the ground, forcing himself forward, desperate for the wire not to touch his back. It was appalling. If it had not been so long since he had eaten, he would certainly have been sick. A vice seemed to be squeezing his head, sending spears of pain from one ear to the other.

All four leopards swung to face him, teeth bared, ears flattened.

He was in the cage. He felt Thoughtcatcher's power escape

from the pain and soar like a song. Behind him, came the tiny thread of Whisper's mind, still weakened by the wire.

As he scrambled to his feet, he saw the look of fury in the leopards' faces softening into one of wonder. Tall Quercus slackened his jaws. His adversary lifted a paw and wiped away the drops of blood. The other two began to relax, loosening their limbs, settling down to the raw meat between their paws. The knucklebone lay on the ground, undisputed.

'Bravo!' A burst of clapping came from the Yadu behind the wire, and from Mina.

'Thank you!' whispered Novan.

'Just don't ask me to do that again for a while.'

Neither Digonez nor Balgo had joined in the applause.

'Impressive,' said the Femarrat lieutenant. 'And potentially dangerous. We were always taught that you Xerappans were no good at sorcery.'

'It isn't sorcery. There's no risk,' said Balgo quickly. 'They couldn't turn the cats against us. There's always a sorcerer on guard ready to kill both of them.'

'It's not the cats as such,' said Digonez, still gazing at Novan. 'It's the power behind it.'

'Can I get out now, sir?' Novan dropped back into the familiar ritual, hanging his head, speaking in a low, expressionless voice, acting the humble servant.

'Yes.'

This time he did retch as he came out under the wire, humiliatingly spitting up yellow bile in front of Alalia. He dared not look up to see how he must disgust her.

'Try it on a human,' Digonez ordered. 'You!' he summoned Mina. 'Now,' to Novan, 'make her jump and croak like a frog.'

Indignation nearly betrayed Novan. Why should he make his sister look a fool for the sport of the Yadu?

'Steady!' warned Thoughtcatcher. *'I'm not going to try, you idiot. He won't know, will he?'*

Novan stared solemnly at Mina. He even tried to bend his own concentration on making her move. There was no piercing song from Thoughtcatcher, surpassing his own will. Besides, he was sure the jerboas didn't have power over humans. Not that sort, anyway. Mina stared back at him. He had an awful feeling that she was trying not to laugh.

'Hmm,' said Digonez finally. 'Maybe you can and maybe you can't. You wouldn't want to give the game away to me, would you? But I think Cozuman should hear about this. Escort Alalia back, will you, Balgo?'

He strode away. Balgo and Alalia looked at each other in dismay.

'Now look what you've done,' said Balgo, 'showing off. Just when we're about to ally ourselves with the most powerful family in Yadu, you have to bring your flaming leopards with you, and a bunch of grubby Xerappans to arouse suspicion.'

'I like that! It was Ma who wanted to make a big impression. And Pa said we mustn't let them think we were a bunch of hicks from the backwoods. And the cats *are* special!' She sounded close to tears.

'I hope that one's not badly hurt. I'd been wondering if we might sell them at a good price if we got someone interested while we're here. It might be the beginning of a lucrative trade.'

'Is that all you can think of? Money? When that beautiful beast is bleeding? And what about Novan? Were you thinking of selling him with the leopards too?'

'Novan?' Her brother sounded genuinely bewildered. Before the Xerappan dropped his eyes he saw the realization dawn in Balgo's face.

'You mean the cat-driver? He has a name, does he?'

'Of course he does. He's a human being, isn't he?'

'We...ell. Technically, of course, I suppose the physical make-up is similar. But you'd hardly put a Xerappan in the same class as us, would you? They were made for servants. I don't imagine they'd know what to do with freedom if they had it. Just as well, under the circumstances.'

We were free once, Novan ground his teeth. We ruled this land.

'I hate Digonez!' Alalia burst out. 'He's so supercilious. Making Novan crawl under that wire, upsetting the leopards, wanting to turn Mina into a frog!'

'Ssh!' Balgo slapped his hand over his sister's mouth. He looked over his shoulder at the other Yadu, who had withdrawn a little distance, as though embarrassed at overhearing their quarrel. 'It's all right,' he called. 'Just betrothal-eve nerves. She must be exhausted from the long journey.'

'How dare you?' Alalia mumbled, tugging at his hands.

The young sorcerer gripped her wrist tightly and began to drag her away. To preserve her shreds of dignity she had to go.

Novan stood seething with indignation at Balgo's treatment of her, but still his heart soared. Alalia knew and cared about him, and about the leopards and Mina.

As the party made their way down the cobbled alley towards the wider road, his sister turned her head from the rear of the group and gave him a delighted grin.

Chapter Eleven

Novan lay in the darkness. A mosquito buzzed around the cat-drivers' hut. It circled his head with an insistent whine, like the thoughts that would not leave him and could end only in pain. Alalia no longer wanted to be betrothed to Digonez. Alalia would be made to promise herself to him. Novan was here on Mount Femarrat, but he would never get close to Cozuman. He could not kill him. He had lost his only chance to tell Mina the plan and give her the poison.

Somewhere behind the mosquito's drone the other boys were still whispering. He did not listen to them. Suddenly the room fell silent. Even the mosquito stopped. Footsteps were approaching along the cobbled road. There was a light outside. Theirs was the last hut.

The door was thrown open, with more force than necessary. Novan did not need to see the newcomers to know they were Yadu. They asserted their dominance over the Xerappans in every action. There were two of them. The light from a spell-rod raked the hut. It came to rest on Novan in the corner. He screwed up his eyes against the glare.

'That's the one. The leopard boy. Get up.'

He obeyed, trying to fight down the fear all Xerappans had of the night-time summons, the unknown fate of the people who disappeared, the rumours of solitary imprisonment, of torture, of unmarked graves.

'Get dressed. Make yourself as presentable as you can,

though you're hardly as beautiful as your leopards.'

'*It's all right.*' The thread of reassurance was coming from Thoughtcatcher. '*He's taking you to Cozuman. This could be your big chance.*'

'I thought you were asleep. Why didn't you warn me?' Novan shot back at him.

It was not difficult for the jerboa to secrete himself in the ankle of Novan's trousers as the boy dressed himself by the narrow beam from the spell-rod. Novan could feel the tenseness of the other boys watching. He hoped their jerboas could pick up something of Thoughtcatcher's foreknowledge. The guards themselves had said nothing yet about where they were taking him. Novan felt a certain smug triumph that he did not need to be told.

But why? And how could Thoughtcatcher be so sure it was safe? Cozuman was the most feared man in all the divided lands of Yadu and Xerappo. What could he want with Novan in the middle of the night? The jerboa was keeping maddeningly silent now.

They stepped out into the cooler air of the roadway. Though the sky hung dark overhead, in the distance there was a red glow, as if thrown up by a far-off town. Novan wondered whether it was as late at night as he had thought. It was hard to tell. Blue-white globes of light ringed the perimeter of Femarrat, but Novan suspected they burned all night.

The Yadu sorcerers strode ahead, taking it for granted that he would follow. They did not appear to think he presented any danger behind them. They're right, ground Novan to himself. They know I can't attack them, and I can't run away. I wouldn't stand a chance.

'*But you* can *attack them,*' came that whisper in his mind, '*if you really want to. You're going to meet Cozuman, after all.*'

'Why?' Novan asked. 'Why me?'

83

The answer came in an abrupt turn of the spell-light. This short side path led to the leopards' cage. Lieutenant Digonez stood there, gazing into it. He turned slowly, as though doing Novan a great favour by acknowledging his presence.

'I told Cozuman about your skill with leopards. He wishes to see for himself.'

'Here?' Novan wondered silently.

'No, you idiot. You go to Lord Cozuman; he doesn't come to you,' Thoughtcatcher countered.

'All of them, sir?' Novan asked aloud.

'One will be sufficient. We don't want to endanger the ladies, if your demonstration goes wrong, do we?'

Ladies? Novan's heart beat faster as he tried to reassemble his thoughts. So not a secret interrogation in a prison cell. It sounded more like a social gathering. 'Ladies' did not suggest female sorcerers, but civilian guests. Surely he must mean Alalia and her mother, the banquet on the eve of her betrothal.

Hope and despair wrestled within his spirit. He almost forgot what the sorcerer was wanting him to do.

'Choose the best one,' Digonez ordered. 'Then bring it out.'

'I'll need a collar and reins, sir.'

'Naturally.'

Novan selected the harness from the cart-store and returned to the Fence-wire. The three sorcerers waited silently.

'You want me to go under?'

'Of course. You don't think we're opening the barrier to let four leopards loose in the dark?'

He had to do it again, to force himself under the power in that wire. He lost half his supper. But once they were through and the pressure lifted he could feel the calm song of Thoughtcatcher making a beauty of the night. The sleepy

84

leopards opened their golden eyes and writhed with pleasure. Novan was astonished that the Yadu could not hear the song, for all their sorcerers' powers.

It was a matter of moments to buckle a jewelled collar round the neck of Almond, the most elegant of the four. Tonight even Novan's hands seemed to take on some of the thrill of Thoughtcatcher's music. She sighed and her coat rippled ecstatically. Novan hoped Digonez and his companions could see this in the spell-light.

But as they approached the wire, not even Thoughtcatcher's mind control could persuade the shivering leopard to crouch down and bear the force of revulsion necessary to get under the barrier.

'You'll have to open it.' Novan was surprised at the authority in his voice.

There was a hesitation as the sorcerer escort queried each other. Digonez nodded. One of the others raised his rod. It began to glow with a yellow light which communicated itself along the wire.

'Enough!' Digonez rapped out.

It was a narrow gap, and still a thread of glowing light hung across it, while the rest of the wire stretched away darkly.

'Come,' Digonez ordered.

Novan was trembling now, his confidence gone. What would happen if he tried to drag the leopard through that line? If the force was still there it would batter Thoughtcatcher's mind so that he could not hold the other leopards. It would madden Almond.

'Hurry up. I don't play games.'

'*He's got to get you both to Cozuman,*' urged Thoughtcatcher. '*You have to trust him.*'

It was hard to believe he could walk through that thread of light unharmed. It was not like the Fence at the frontier, which had folded aside. But he was going forward, and

Almond was still obedient at his heel. Thoughtcatcher was in control. Novan wasn't feeling sick. They were through.

There were more and more people as they began to climb the lower slopes of the mountain. The darkness of the drivers' hut and the glare along the perimeter Fence had given way to softer, more welcoming lamps in a residential area. They caught the low-hanging fronds of foliage spilling over courtyard walls, flowers around doorways. Clearly in this inner area the sorcerers felt more secure. People, some in the red uniform of the Guard, many not, lingered on steps or were glimpsed through gateways. They spilled out of bars, enjoying the cool of the night.

Novan and Almond caused something of a sensation. The leopard paced at his heels, beautifully behaved, scorning the stares and whistles which followed her. Digonez and his companions too were silent, though grimmer. None of them answered the shouted calls and questions.

They passed beyond this belt of life and laughter. The hillside was bare now, steeper. Novan's blood quickened. He began to see the rocks of the mountain close up, in the light of the lamps spaced out along the path. By night, it did not have that intense whiteness, which had made it seem like a fairy mountain from a distance. Was it only the lamps which touched it with pale blue? It soared out of sight, ribbed and ridged like the fossilized carcass of some fabulous monster. The shadows between its spines held fissures unfathomably deep.

Now, suddenly, the texture of the road changed under his feet. Digonez cried out a warning as Novan almost stumbled. Almond let out a hiss.

There was a step in front of him. It was not clean-cut, but rounded at its edge as though worn by water. Indeed, as he looked down, the steps themselves might have been made of frozen liquid. Deep green, streaked with black, and almost translucent. Darker lines and flaws appeared to be trapped within the stone, like insects in amber.

The steps were quite high, the surface treacherously smooth. Climbing them demanded care. For once the agile Almond seemed awkward. She struggled to position her four paws on a stair-tread not quite wide enough for the length of her body. Novan recalled the party he had seen from far off, climbing this green waterfall of stone towards Cozuman's house. One did not easily come at the High Sorcerer, nor escape in a hurry.

After a while he paused to draw his breath and look back. He could see the little township they had passed through, the starker lines of the barracks below, stripped of trees, the perimeter Fence, brightly lit. A softer farmland beyond, showing barely a light at this late hour, away to the distant glow of a city by the sea. No glint of waves now. The moon had not risen yet. Yadu was peaceful, half asleep.

Femarrat would never sleep. This was the heart of power. It must keep beating. And at the centre of all things, Cozuman. If Cozuman died...

'Don't loiter. Lord Cozuman doesn't like to be kept waiting.'

The steps felt steeper now. His legs ached.

There were no trees around Cozuman's house. A wide, white space had been hacked from the mountain into a raw terrace. Novan felt that it had not been there long. The Yadu had imposed this upon a mountain once worshipped in its natural perfection. Like their temple on the summit.

All at once there were many guards, emerging out of the shadows into the white space. They seemed to be expecting Digonez and his strange charges. As Novan led his leopard through their ranks they stared silently, but no less curiously than the noisy revellers below.

He was sure there would be another Fence, but there was not. It made Novan feel uneasy, rather than reassured. Would there be some different barrier he was as yet unaware of? Thoughtcatcher had gone silent. Novan felt a chill of fear. Did the jerboa suspect that the High Sorcerer of Yadu might have more subtle means of detection than his Sorcerer Guard used elsewhere? Would he know if Thoughtcatcher communicated with Novan? If he did, it would mean that the little jerboa would be separated from him in an instant and killed. Even worse, all their jerboas would be killed. The only advantage the Xerappans had over the Children of Yadu would be betrayed and exterminated.

Could Cozuman read thoughts? Novan tried to stop himself thinking of the slip of poison in his shirt collar. But the more he tried not to, the more it dominated his mind. How was he to cut the stitching and get it out, without anyone seeing? How could he get close enough to Cozuman's food or drink to use it? What would happen if he did – to himself, to Mina, to all the Xerappans?

The door was opening on a golden interior. Music wafted out, the lingering smell of meat and spices, the sound of falling water, and human voices. A girl's laughter. Alalia?

Almost without his realizing it, they were steering him across the courtyard. There were tables set out in the open air. The food had been cleared away, except for platters of jewel-like fruit and jugs of wine. A bewildering motley of men and women were seated around them. In his confusion he could not identify Alalia.

But a figure rose from the head of the central table, and at once he dominated all Novan's mind. A sorcerer in a white robe with an edge of crimson. Taller than was common, even for a Yadu. Long hair drawn back behind his ears to reveal a chiselled face. A voice which spoke low, but with an unquestioned authority.

'Welcome back, Digonez. So this is your fiancée's entertainment?'

Lord Cozuman. The most hated and the most feared of all the Children of Yadu. Cozuman, who had slaughtered a whole Xerappan village of men, women and children, to panic the rest into fleeing for the hills. Cozuman, who had strung his magic Fence across the pass, turning the fertile half of Xerappo into the land of Yadu, who was now planting colonies even in the hills beyond, to which the Xerappans had fled. Cozuman, who claimed the sacred heart of Xerappo for the headquarters of his Sorcerer Guard.

Novan stood face to face with the High Sorcerer of Yadu, who was studying him critically from head to toe.

Chapter Twelve

Lord Cozuman stretched out his hand. The rod he held was so much more small and delicate than those of the uniformed Guard. Novan did not even see it until the last moment. Then he felt its power. The air between them vibrated with an unearthly green, tinged with yellow. As it writhed over him, Novan wanted to twist away, to flee, to cower in hiding, but he could not move. Inside, he felt he was trembling to the point of collapse, yet his body was held rigid.

Almond began to move restively. She pawed the ground. Had Thoughtcatcher been immobilized too by the searching beam? For a moment, the leopard seemed too surprised to know what to do with her freedom.

Then the beam snapped off. The rod was slipped back into Cozuman's sleeve. To his intense relief, Novan heard within him the soaring song of Thoughtcatcher. He knew that Almond must be hearing it too and falling back under its spell.

'You were very afraid,' said Cozuman, still in that low, amused voice. 'Most afraid of all when I probed around your neck. I was receiving levels of reaction unusually high for your appearance here as a minor player at a social gathering. Did you think we would hang you? That is not quite the entertainment I had in mind for my guests. Hardly appropriate for a betrothal-eve party... Search him!'

Digonez looked startled, and stepped forward in protest,

as though he were being accused of some dereliction of duty. Two of Cozuman's house-guards seized Novan. They ran ungentle hands over his neck and shoulders and armpits. Their grip fell away; they shrugged their shoulders.

'Nothing, my lord.'

'No pendant round his neck? No weapon under his arm? No phial of poison hidden in a pocket inside his shirt? The Xerappans are rather fond of poison. It suits their low and twisted natures. It appears to be the only means they can think of to use against us, apart from boys throwing stones.'

Novan felt the blood pounding in his ears. Cozuman knew, and yet he didn't quite know enough. The guards had apparently been feeling for a phial of metal or glass, or a tablet that would resist their fingers. The softness of Grandmother Roann's cylinder of powder encased in skin, stitched into the partly-yielding stuff of his collar, had deceived them.

But Cozuman was not quite satisfied. The voice was gentler than ever, the eyes hooded to narrow slits. 'Why, boy? Why were you so afraid?'

Novan grabbed at a partial truth. 'It was when the light got near my head, sir. I have to control the leopard. It's all done by thought. I knew if you numbed my brain I couldn't hold her. And I was right. If you hadn't taken the light off, she might have...' He looked sideways. The leopard had slithered down into a relaxed position, hind legs drawn under her, front paws stretched out. But her intelligent head was still questing round the scene, her nostrils twitching at the lingering scent of meat.

'I see...' Cozuman was silent for a while, perhaps surprised at so simple an explanation. Novan wished Thoughtcatcher would tell him what was going on in the High Sorcerer's mind. Yet another part of him was glad for the silence. He was aware that the risks of discovery were far greater here than elsewhere in Yadu.

'Well... Alalia Yekhavu, come forward. You are our guest of honour.'

Digonez crossed to the table and held out his hand. Alalia rose. Novan had hardly dared look before. She was dressed in pale yellow, an intricately pleated dress that fell loose from her bare shoulders, just caught at the waist by a golden girdle. Mina must have spent ages curling her naturally straight hair. It was swept up by a gold comb and then tumbled in waves down the back of the yellow dress. Tiny gold slippers peeped from under the gold-fringed, sweeping skirt. She looked frightened.

Anger swept through Novan as he saw Digonez's hand close possessively round her fingers. The lieutenant led her forward to stand before Cozuman. The High Sorcerer smiled.

'Don't be afraid, child. You come as a delightful refreshment to a military base. And you've brought us an exotic diversion. We have no leopards in the plains. As a caged animal alone, this one would be a beautiful spectacle. But it appears your cats are more than a menagerie exhibit. I am told you have domesticated the Xerappans too and harnessed one of their more outlandish talents. What can you make this pair do?'

Digonez was laughing, at Alalia's side. Alalia was staring at Novan, mutely, unhappily. This was what he had been reduced to in her eyes: a performing animal. Probably this was all she had ever seen him as. Something less than human.

She was speaking now, in a strained, scared voice. 'We don't really use them for entertainment, my lord. Just to draw chariots and things. You know the hill country isn't suitable for horses. They get sick. And when we found out that leopards and lions could be trained to do it ... They look so elegant...' Her voice trailed away breathlessly.

This was not the Alalia that Novan remembered. That

confident, laughing girl who had been the envy of all the younger children at the Colony. The girl Novan had watched with longing at the edge of the swimming pool. The girl who had declared only a few hours ago that she no longer wanted to marry Digonez.

Cozuman subjected her to that same searching scrutiny he had given Novan. He sounded impatient. 'Digonez, I thought you suggested this ability might have security implications.'

'Yes, sir. If these beasts are really under the Xerappans' control, they could be ordered to attack us.'

'And you think one lift of a sorcerer's rod wouldn't slay them on the spot and deliver their handlers to a slower death?'

'But if no sorcerer was around...'

'Do the Children of Yadu go anywhere in Xerappo without a guard? And there are no leopards here in Yadu.'

'There is one now. In the house of the High Sorcerer.'

There was a gasp from around the table. Novan felt the force of hostile eyes all focused on him. But Cozuman laughed. 'I don't feel as threatened as you seem to think I should. I repeat, claws and teeth are no match for magic. Still, a demonstration might be diverting ... You!' The hooded lids rose. The eyes wide, brilliant with intensity, stared into Novan's face. 'Make your leopard attack me.'

Novan choked. 'But I wouldn't, sir! You said you'd kill her! I can't!'

'Do it.' The hand was rising, the rod creeping forward out of his sleeve, like the golden head of a snake emerging. Novan began to hear a singing in his ears, more terrible than Thoughtcatcher's magical air. His will was turning to water. His heart was breaking for what would happen to Almond.

'No!' shouted Alalia. 'Novan, don't do it!'

'Be quiet!' Cozuman snapped the order, but it was Digonez who drew his rod and pointed it at Alalia, holding his fiancée of tomorrow rigid under his spell.

Novan had almost forgotten that it was not he who was in control of the leopard. He never had been. That was only the outward show, for the benefit of the Yadu. In the confusion of his mind he felt the calming song of Thoughtcatcher grow sharper, more intense. Almond's coat rippled menacingly. Her claws sprang out from their sandy-gold sheaths. She was rising to her feet, muscles taut, gathering her body for the spring. Cozuman tensed. His spell-rod was fully in his hand. Every guard had his out, trained on that narrow space between the leopard and the High Sorcerer.

'Don't... any of you... interfere.' Cozuman's order was almost too soft to be heard, but the other rods wavered and fell. 'Now!'

The leopard sprang – but not straight at Cozuman's throat. She leaped high into the air. The High Sorcerer's rod flashed its vivid green light, accompanied by a curse too horrible to hear. It struck the empty air chest-high, where he had expected Almond to come. There was a crackling explosion. Novan winced as the shock wave struck him with searing heat.

A split second later, Almond spun a somersault higher than the sorcerer's head and landed soft-footed in front of the astonished Cozuman. Instantly she lay down, her head submissive between her two front paws. Her ears flattened.

The High Sorcerer stared down at her, and then up at the equally astonished Novan. 'Fool! I wouldn't have killed such a valuable animal, merely stunned her. Why did you do that? ... *How* did you do that?'

Novan shrugged, assuming an expression of stupidity he had often found useful. 'I didn't want to hurt anybody, sir. I thought it would be less dangerous all round. And she's a beautiful jumper.' He could feel the tremor of Thoughtcatcher's laughter.

The brilliant eyes, narrowed again, were still staring at him.

Novan felt that gaze was more dangerous than the probing spell-light. 'Hmm. You did right to show me this, Digonez. There is more here than the drawing of chariots, whatever your pretty fiancée suggests. The minds of the Xerappans are perhaps not quite as oafish as we would like to believe.' There was a flash in those black pupils that for a moment was pure hatred. Novan recoiled. Almond uttered a growl, instantly suppressed. 'Take him away. I'll talk to him later, when you've loosened his tongue.'

Hands seized Novan. Two burly sorcerers marched him away. He twisted his head to see what would happen to Almond. The leopard rose and padded after him. His mind was whirling. They were taking him to a prison cell to torture him. They would break him until he told them everything: the jerboas, the plan to assassinate Cozuman, his family's part in the resistance. Somehow he had to get the poison out of his collar and swallow it himself. If he could not kill Cozuman, then at least he must die rather than betray his people.

Chapter Thirteen

He tried to hold his head high as he was marched past the staring guests seated around the tables. He must not show them his terror. He dared not look at Alalia, though he heard her soft cry. Dimly, through the fears that were roaring in his head, he was aware of something like another quiver of laughter from Thoughtcatcher. It was doubly scary that even the jerboa was giving way to hysteria. He had depended so much on him for wisdom and warning.

Beyond the light of the tall lamps around the tables the guards halted. Novan struggled to refocus his eyes. There was starlight here, in the further reaches of the huge courtyard, some pools of lamplight from the house windows. The shadows were trickier. A murmur of voices, in front of him, not behind.

Novan licked dry lips. There would be a doorway, probably steps down. Cozuman's torture chamber must be underground, out of sight, out of hearing of the party guests. There was a tree overhanging this corner of the courtyard. He breathed deep lungfuls of pine-scented air. This was the last time he would smell such freshness.

'Sit down.'

The edge of a bench jarred his knee. He was aware of the indrawn breath of several people, quite close to him.

'Can't you understand Yaduan? I said, sit.'

He clambered over the bench seat. There was a trestle-table. The sorcerers' hands forced him down. One of them picked up the shadowy bulk of a wine jug and thumped it down before him. Then a beaker. He heard the trickle of liquid being poured. He had not realized how much his hand was shaking until the guard forced the cup into it and ordered him to drink. The other dimly-seen people around the table had fallen very still.

Was this how it ended? They were not waiting for him to take his own poison.

It tasted like wine. He was so scared he thought he would gag at the first mouthful and cough it back. But he made himself swallow.

He found to his surprise that he felt better. He drank some more. Someone was refilling his cup. The guards had withdrawn a little.

A smaller hand touched his.

'It's Mina,' signalled Thoughtcatcher hastily, before either of them could give their knowledge of each other away.

He gripped her fingers tightly. He still could not understand what was happening. Mina's jerboa Whisper silently explained. *'Pakann is here too. Alalia's mother's demanded that both Yekhavu ladies be allowed to bring their maids, in case they needed attention to their hair or dresses. But there are some of Cozuman's servants at this table, so be careful. They're Yadu.'*

'Then they don't have jerboas,' crowed Thoughtcatcher.

Novan turned his head. It seemed impossible that the two sorcerers couldn't hear this clear communication that was passing between the Xerappans. One of them bent to fill a jug from the waist-high jar that was standing in front of some bushes near the table.

'Just wine,' giggled Thoughtcatcher. *'There's more than one way of loosening tongues.'*

'You *knew*?'

'*Ssh! Or they'll wonder why you're getting so angry.*'

'I'll deal with you later.'

Novan set down his beaker. In the hugeness of his relief he had drunk two cupfuls already. He must be more careful. Cozuman had indicated that he still wanted to question him further. Probably when this party was over.

'Is there any water?' his mind asked Whisper.

Mina reached for a different pitcher and refilled his cup.

As his mind cleared, Novan watched a servant come from the lamplit guest tables and dip two more jugs into the wine jar. As she bore them back, there was a burst of singing and laughter.

Novan froze. Coldly, certainly, he saw what he had to do. He could never get close to Cozuman unwatched. But the wine that Cozuman was drinking came from that jar.

Was it already too late? How much longer would this party last? Might those be the last jugs drawn for the High Sorcerer's table?

There was a hiss from under the bench. He had not even noticed the leopard sprawled at his feet.

Mina turned her head quickly, thinking something was wrong. But Novan's hopes were soaring. This was his chance. If he acted swiftly enough... He could be the hero of Xerappo. He would go down in history as the boy who killed the High Sorcerer of Yadu, the hated Cozuman, in his own house, and set his people free.

'Have you got a knife?' His mind conveyed the question to Mina through her jerboa.

'Of course not. They searched us on the way in. And they took our table knives away when they cleared the plates.'

'Are your nails sharp enough to cut through Grandmother's stitching?'

'Would scissors do?'

'Why didn't you say!'

98

'We had to bring their vanity cases and a sewing kit, didn't we? We're ladies' maids.'

Novan glanced across at his guards. They had seated themselves at the end of the table. They were chatting, apparently relaxed. But he was disturbingly aware of the rods which hung at their belts, within instant reach.

'There's something sewn into my collar. At the front, on the left.' If minds could whisper softer than breathing, his would have. 'I need to get it out without anyone seeing.'

Mina leaned across the table. Her movements were languid, a little clumsy, as though she were drunk. Laughing unsteadily, she picked up the pitcher of water and slopped some of it into his beaker and more on the table. Pakann, catching her intention, was trying to do the same for the guards with the jug of wine, but they waved her away. Cozuman's household sorcerers did not drink on duty.

Mina's arm draped itself round Novan's neck. She leaned her head on his shoulder. One of the guards laughed. 'You've made a hit there, leopard boy! Better watch your big cat doesn't get jealous.'

How much could they see in the starlight?

He felt his sister's other hand creeping up his chest. It was at his throat. The slightest shock of cold metal. He bent his head lower over hers, shielding her fingers and the tiny scissors they held. Once he almost cried out as the points nipped his skin. She was working blind, probing the inside seam against his neck. He longed to beg her to be careful, terrified she would slit the package, and was taken by surprise at her immediate, cross response, 'I'm being as careful as I can.' They could not hide their thoughts from each other, as long as Thoughtcatcher and Whisper were active.

She withdrew the scissors. Her small finger felt for the gap she had made, and began to work the cylinder out. Instantly his hand went up, replacing hers.

'Sorry!' she signalled indignantly. 'That's it, is it?'

'This is more dangerous than you know.' So the jerboas weren't telling her everything.

Her protest fell silent. Novan felt through Whisper a glow of warmth from his sister, a realization that she was being included in something risky and momentous, though she still did not know what.

Novan's own finger found the cylindrical packet wrapped in fine skin. He eased it out of its hiding place. His forefinger and thumb enveloped it. None of the Yadu had seen.

'Mina!'

The guards jumped to attention. Mina and Pakann had risen. Novan tore his mind away from the cylinder of grommalan powder and turned more slowly.

Alalia was standing a little distance off. Her yellow dress seemed to illuminate this darker space. Around the guest tables, other people had got to their feet. Clearly something was about to happen. Was this the end? Were they going?

'I want my cloak,' Alalia ordered. 'Cozuman has arranged a witch-light display to round off the party, and it's getting cooler.'

'*Why didn't she send a servant?*' Thoughtcatcher and Whisper were querying each other.

A moment later, Thoughtcatcher told Novan, '*I fancy she'd like to talk to you.*'

Novan's mind was racing. What could Alalia Yekhavu possibly want to say to him, here in front of servants and house-guards? Could it have anything to do with that moment at the leopard cage, when she had told her brother defiantly that Novan was a human being and that she hated Digonez? If only she had a jerboa, so that they could speak to each other in silence!

But a more insistent thought was communicating itself to him through his fingers. The packet of poison. His one unrepeatable chance. Now, in this flurry of movement, as guests were rising from the tables, he could get close to the wine jar. Surely, with the night growing colder and the finale still to come, Cozuman and his guests would want another round of drinks to warm them?

He began to edge away from the table towards the jar.

Mina had disappeared, but now came running back with something soft and darker than Alalia's dress. She had to stand on tiptoe to arrange it around the Yadu girl's shoulders.

Novan reached his free hand behind him. The leaves of the bushes rustled. He found the edge of the wine jar.

Pakann was hurrying across the space to the central lamplight with a cloak for Emania Yekhavu. Cozuman was ushering his guests into position around the fountain.

'So much more magical to see the light reflected in water.' His voice, though he never seemed to raise it, came clearly across the courtyard.

Water, thought Novan bitterly. You stole ours. Our rivers are hardly more than a trickle, though there used to be leaping waterfalls and deep pools. You dive into your swimming pools and waste it in fountains, while our crops shrivel.

Now was his chance. Now he could get back, not just at Cozuman, but at all of them. Digonez, the Sorcerer Guard, these privileged guests drinking and enjoying themselves on the Xerappans' sacred mountain, Alalia's supercilious brother Balgo... His nails were starting to slit the wrapping. It would only take a second to empty the powder into the wine. Enough, he knew, to kill everyone here and hundreds more.

'*And Alalia,*' Thoughtcatcher put in. '*You mustn't forget her.*'

Alalia? Novan was shocked out of the euphoria that he was about to do what everyone in the Xerappan resistance movement had longed to do, yet could not: kill Cozuman.

101

Not Alalia, not her!

She was only a few steps away. Her pale face gazed at him over the soft, dark cloak.

The powder was starting to spill out of his trembling fingers. He snatched the packet back into his clenched fist. Had any of the grains gone into the jar, or had they tumbled harmlessly down to the ground?

Alalia? Could he kill her too? If that was the price to eliminate Cozuman. To remove Digonez, his nephew. To assassinate in one night the most feared sorcerers of the Yadu regime. Was Alalia's death the price he had to pay for Xerappo's freedom?

A remembered voice rang with the grief of his grandparents. 'He killed the whole of the village of Sea Pines. The Sorcerer Guard didn't spare anyone, men, women or babies. No fate is too bad for him, for all the Children of Yadu. They took our land when we fled, our farms, our homes.' He remembered the front-door key in the withered fingers of Grandmother Roann, the home she would never be allowed to go back to.

Alalia was a Child of Yadu. Could he blame her for that?

'Killing the innocents. That's what Cozuman does. You could become like him.'

'Like Cozuman? Me?'

'If you want to.'

He stared at the white blur of Alalia's face. His fingers slowly unclenched. The grommalan poison trickled noiselessly down the outside of the wine jar.

Chapter Fourteen

Novan stood shocked and motionless. Then he snatched a handful of leaves from the flower-bed behind him and frantically scoured the curve of the jar. His heel ground the polluted remains into the earth beneath the bushes. He scrubbed at his hands as well. He was breathing fast, horrified by how close he had come to a murder too awful to think about.

But an accusing voice was railing at him too: You've betrayed them all – your grandparents, Father, Big Knife. You had this one chance and now you've blown it.

There was an eddy of movement from the corners of the courtyard, where members of Cozuman's household had been waiting in the shadows. Everyone was flocking to that central lighted space around the fountain. Abruptly, the lights went out. There was an immediate, startling contrast between the darkness enclosed now by the protecting walls of Cozuman's house and the more distant glare of the security lamps that scanned the approaches to it. Many of the guests gasped. Novan realized that families like the Yekhavus would have little experience of real darkness in their guarded colonies, and were frightened by it.

This darkness was not, of course, total. It was only the sudden contrast which made it seem so. There was starlight, such as he and Mina were used to. The harsh lights beyond the house leaked something of their brilliance even inside these walls. He looked down. Almond's eyes glowed with their own green luminousness.

'Move it!' urged one of his guards. 'I bet you've never seen a witch-light show before.'

He allowed himself, unresisting, to be shepherded forward with the rest.

He had hardly reached the back of the crowd when a whoosh of green fire shot into the sky. At first it seemed like a fan of coloured flame, but as it rose it took on the skirt, the torso, the outstretched arms, the flowing hair of a woman with red eyes. She was writhing, dancing, stooping low over their heads. People screamed and backed away as she raked her nails through their hair in an explosion of sparks. Novan's guards jumped on to a vacated bench for a better look. Novan was torn between instinctive amazement at the sight and the overwhelming thoughts of what had nearly happened, and now never would. He was still not certain he had made the right choice, but he could not bear to imagine the alternative. He would have poisoned Alalia.

Another sheet of flame, salmon pink this time. To gasps of astonishment, it solidified into a pair of elephants with purple tusks. Novan had never seen such beasts, but he recognized them from stories of the trains of pilgrims who had once streamed to Mount Femarrat bearing gifts to Xerappo from the far south. The green witch was dancing with the elephants, somersaulting from one broad back to the other. As they lowered their tusks and fanned their enormous ears, blasts of heat drove the onlookers apart. The crowd was pressing back around Novan, growing increasingly scared. He heard Cozuman laugh.

Darkness fell again. There was apprehension, as well as anticipation, now.

Something brushed Novan's face, like a giant moth. He bit back a cry. What new devilry was this?

A voice spoke, no more than a murmur. 'Novan? I saw your leopard's eyes. It is you, isn't it?'

'Alalia?' His lips shaped her name without sound.

A gush of brilliant blue became a swan flying over their heads uttering desolate cries. From her dropped glittering eggs. People ducked away, until they realized what those eggs were. Then they rushed forward. The eggs fell into the forest of grasping hands as solid rubies.

Novan ignored the sport. In the renewal of light he saw that Alalia had withdrawn a few prudent paces. She was wrapped in a cloak of soft, grey feathers that almost hid her yellow dress. Now it fell open as she reached up her hands with the rest, laughing a little breathlessly. She plucked a jewel out of the sky, like the honoured guest she was.

Again the light died. The yellow dress was hidden by the cloak. Alalia was at his side, breathing in his ear. 'You have to help me. I can't bear to marry Digonez. But I'm frightened of Cozuman. If I stay till tomorrow, he'll make me go through with this betrothal. I have to get away.'

'What can I do about that? I'm his prisoner!' It was hard to keep the bitterness in his voice to a whisper.

Red light was encircling the whole courtyard now. People turned and gasped in horror. They were caught in a ring of flame. Even as they watched, the flames took on faces and hands. Leering, grinning at them. Crimson and scarlet imps cavorted in a ring that was creeping ever nearer. The guests huddled closer, unsure what would happen when their shrinking centre of darkness was invaded.

Alalia's feathered cloak was pressed close against Novan. She was not watching the demons. 'You have some power. I know you do. The way you handle the leopards. And you have...'

'*The jerboa,*' put in Thoughtcatcher proudly.

'The jerboa...' Alalia's whisper rose higher. 'So *that's* what

105

that voice is!'

'You *know*? You heard him?' Novan was shocked into incredulity. 'But... you're a Yadu.'

She was staring into his eyes in the crimson light. 'Are we so utterly different, the Children of Yadu and Xerappans? I'm a human being too.'

'I know that!' Somehow he had hold of her hand. He ached to tell her that he had just saved her life, but he was too appalled at what else he would have to confess before that.

The red glare was becoming more intense, the menacing circle of goblins whirling round them as they advanced from all sides. They were grimacing, mimicking the dance of the green witch who was swooping overhead. Alalia broke away from Novan as the light intensified where they stood.

'So there you are!' Her brother Balgo was at her elbow, in the dress uniform of the Sorcerer Guard, a white tunic with borders of crimson. 'Digonez is furious. You're supposed to be the guest of honour, and you just disappeared.'

'I'm sorry. That witch scared me. I tried to dodge out of her way and then I got trapped in the crowd. But I caught this ruby from the swan.' She held out her hand and stared. It was empty, only stained with red liquid.

Balgo dashed it away. 'You ran away from witch-light? It's not real. None of this is. You didn't think so, did you? Do you want to make us appear like provincial ninnies?'

Alalia looked doubtfully at the leering faces of goblins. The red eyes in the ring around her were growing larger and larger. 'Why does Cozuman like frightening people so? Is this his idea of a pleasant entertainment for my betrothal-eve party?'

'Ssh! Suppose somebody heard you? You don't question Lord Cozuman's decisions. He's the High Sorcerer. He has to look fierce. If it wasn't for him, there wouldn't *be* a land of Yadu. The Xerappans would drive us all into the sea, if they didn't kill us first.'

'As we drove *them* into the hills, or killed them?' asked Alalia softly.

Novan was close enough to hear every word they said. He had had a lifetime of trying to remain invisible, to stay out of trouble. He concentrated now on keeping utterly still, head bowed, even quietening his mind. Anything to avoid Balgo noticing his presence.

It is more difficult to overlook a leopard. Balgo's gaze fell on the cat and then lifted to her handler.

'You?' His look darted from Novan to Alalia and back again. 'So you couldn't find your fiancé in the crowd, but you had no difficulty bumping into your cat-driver.'

There was no time to say more. The red goblins leaped upon them. Balgo might deride them as an illusion, but there was heat on Novan's arms, clawed fingers pulling at his hair, demonic laughter in his ears. Yet it was not him but Alalia they wanted. He heard her shriek. The writhing circle ringed her in fire. The goblins had passed over everyone else and were dancing round her. They grabbed her feathered cloak from her shoulders, so that she stood out slender and pale within a spinning circle of flames. Her face was terrified. Novan tried to press forward to help her, but hands held him back. These were human hands. Cozuman's guards, detailed to mind him, were on either side.

Powerless to stop it, he watched the fire demons lift the helpless Alalia up on a spinning vortex and carry her over the heads of the fast-scattering crowd. Digonez stood waiting by the fountain, with Cozuman at his side. Slowly the flames subsided. Alalia was deposited to stand in front of the two sorcerers. The circle of fire was sinking lower, the red goblins crouching, dwindling.

'That was an illusion?' Novan cried, turning on Balgo. 'They picked her up and carried her!'

107

Balgo smiled thinly. 'Oh, there is certainly power here, but it's not in the things you think you see.'

Alalia and Digonez were standing now in a shallow sea of scarlet. They were too far away for Novan to read the expressions in their faces as they looked at each other. He thought from Alalia's bearing that she was tense and quivering from fear, or anger. Digonez looked more at ease, probably smiling. He was sure Cozuman was. How could they do this to her, the night before her betrothal? Unless it was to prove that Digonez would have absolute power over her, once she was his. As his uncle Lord Cozuman had power over all of them, Yadu and Xerappans.

But something was happening to that sea of scarlet. Where were the grimacing goblins, the twisting flames? There was a different movement now, swirling upwards, sprouting tongues of fiery red that were no longer burning. The gasps all around the crowd were of wonder, not of terror. Digonez and Alalia stood face to face amid a field of poppies. As the bell-like heads swayed, their silken petals sang with unearthly music, as if clouds of nightingales were drifting across the stars. There was a scent, like nothing Novan had ever experienced before. It slowed his racing heart, calmed his breathing. Terror receded; he had almost forgotten it already. A soft hand caressed his mind, soothing his anger and indignation, as it smoothed the furrows from his brow. It had all been an illusion. Nothing was wrong. Digonez loved Alalia. He would be betrothed to her tomorrow and take care of her for ever. All would be well.

'*If you believe that, you'll believe anything,*' came a sharp thought from somewhere near his feet.

Chapter Fifteen

A river of gold was carrying the guests to the gates, while nightingales rained down song out of the darkness overhead. Every one of the visitors had their arm round someone. They were smiling contentedly. Cozuman's party had been a great success. Many of them were singing, not drunkenly, but sleepily. They had completely forgotten how they had been terrorized, horrified, for Cozuman's sport. Only the beautiful things remained in their minds.

Alalia was leaning on Digonez's shoulder as the lieutenant saw her back to her lodgings. She looked happy, though just a little puzzled. There were poppy petals in her hair.

But for Novan, the spell had been broken. 'Speak to her, now that we know she can hear you!' he ground at the jerboa. 'She mustn't go through with it. She's seen what he's like. She can't have forgotten already!'

'*Not here. Not yet,*' the jerboa warned him.

Mina was passing them. The golden tide that looked like water, but was not, lapped round her ankles. She turned her head. Novan saw her eyes struggling to hold on to consciousness. He knew that Whisper must be speaking to her, recalling her to reality.

'She needs you.' He felt his sister's sudden, clear communication.

'I know. But what can I *do*?'

'*There are secrets under Femarrat. Ways that should not*

be spoken of.' This time it came from Thoughtcatcher, not Mina's mind.

Brother and sister looked down. The jerboa had emerged on to Novan's boot, a brown pebble in a sea of gold. The light was reflected warmly in his round eyes. He drew his tiny forelegs up under his chin.

Novan was torn between fear that a sorcerer would see him and reassurance at this visible, furry evidence that they still had help.

'What do you mean?' his mind whispered, while Mina stared.

'*Not here. Not yet.*' Then sharply to Mina, '*Tell your mistress to stay alert. We may only have one chance.*'

Mina and Whisper were being carried past Novan. It was impossible for a Xerappan maid to stay behind without attracting attention. An emptiness overtook Novan as the Yekhavu party left the courtyard. He felt Thoughtcatcher nudge back inside his trouser leg. Something else stirred and yawned as the golden tide ebbed. He had forgotten about the leopard.

He had almost forgotten the guards too. Now, alone, with the illusion gone and normal lamplight replacing the witch-flames, he remembered what he was doing here and why he was being held. Cozuman wanted to question him.

It seemed long ago that he had sat with the servants, and Mina had poured him water instead of wine. His head should have stayed clear, but it was reeling with memories, any one of which was enough to overwhelm him.

He had nearly carried out his plan to poison the wine and fulfil his mission to kill Cozuman... and with him Alalia and everyone else. He had experienced the terror and the beauty of Cozuman's party tricks, his senses like clay in the High Sorcerer's hands. He had heard a heart-rending plea from Alalia to save her from this betrothal, and then seen her

110

restored to Digonez. Thoughtcatcher had hinted that there was still a way out, one single, unrepeatable opportunity, between now and tomorrow's binding ceremony. And he had not the faintest idea what it was.

Left with his fear and doubt, and his sense of his own inadequacy, he could hardly stand. The guards led him back to the fountain, where Cozuman still stood. The leopard followed at his heels.

The High Sorcerer turned his head. His thin face looked tired. Novan knew little about the exercise of sorcery, but he guessed that the spells needed for such a fantastic display must have drained his strength. It was a small satisfaction to know that he was human. Cozuman seemed to draw himself together with an effort.

'So, boy. Whatever little skill you Xerappans have with leopards and lions, you see it couldn't stand for one second against the sorcery of the Yadu.'

'No, sir.'

'How do you do it?'

'Do what, sir?'

'Don't play games. You're far from stupid, so don't pretend to be.'

'How do I control the leopard, you mean, sir? I'm not sure I really know myself. I just sort of *think*, really hard, and usually it seems to work. The cats do what I want.'

'Does it work on other animals, besides leopards and lions?'

'I... I'm not really sure, sir. I don't think so. We don't need that sort of control for any others. Horses don't usually survive long in the hill country, and if they did, they'd be manageable by normal means, wouldn't they? Like camels.'

'You find camels manageable?' Cozuman might have been smiling.

'Not difficult enough to need that kind of thought control,

111

anyway, sir. Balgo Yekhavu manages his well enough.'

'But you wouldn't object to a little experiment?'

'N... no.' He could not help his heart racing faster as Cozuman's smile widened.

The High Sorcerer gave a flick of his hand. Immediately an officer was at his side, bearing a small box. He set it down on the table in front of his master.

'Open it.' The sorcerer, who wore the orange epaulettes of a captain, flinched. He seemed to have to force himself to reach forward, unlock the clasp and lift the lid. At once, he started back.

There was darkness in the box. They all watched. Slowly the darkness clotted and enlarged itself. Something was hauling itself up over the lip of the box. Something the size of Novan's fist.

The High Sorcerer reached out his hand. His small, slender rod was poised now between his fingertips. It glowed with white light, just faintly yellow. Carefully he advanced it to the edge of the box until its glow illuminated the black, furred body, the crooked legs of a very large spider.

Novan's muscles screamed at him to back away, but sorcerers stood behind him, blocking flight.

Cozuman gently inserted his rod under the spider. It clung dangerously to the gold tip. The High Sorcerer rose, balancing his dark burden delicately. He came towards Novan.

'You do well to look afraid,' he said softly. 'She has enough poison in her jaws to kill a dozen Xerappans.'

'Help me!' Novan's mind screamed at Thoughtcatcher.

'Sorry. Jerboas don't do spiders. You're on your own.'

'What am I going to do? Don't leave me!'

'I think doing absolutely nothing might be the best bet.'

The rod was descending towards Novan's arm. He watched with horror as the bloated body was deposited on his sleeve, a black clot on the creamy fabric. There was a moment's stillness. The spider began to crawl towards Novan's neck.

It was heavy enough for him to feel its progress through the fabric of his shirt. He found himself willing it to stop, to freeze, as though his own mind really could control other creatures. Still it was working its way up, above his elbow now. Its feet hooked in the rough cloth, dragging it down as it hauled its heavy body higher and higher. It would reach his shoulder soon. Only the corner of his eye could see it. He dared not move the rigid muscles of his neck.

It was high on his left arm. It was moving inwards now, on to his shoulder blade, just below his chin. The collar of his shirt hung open, where Mina had cut the stitching to remove the packet of poison. He was bitterly aware of the irony, that it should be this very spot where the spider's jaws would strike and this other poison enter his own body. Did Cozuman know everything? Had he planned this?

The High Sorcerer was watching intently.

The first leg flicked Novan's bare skin. His throat contracted. He could see the head now, separate from the big black body heaving itself up over the rim of his collar. He was aware of two gleaming eyes, of a coarse fuzz of hair illuminated against the glow of Cozuman's spell-rod.

Beneath the eyes he glimpsed a mouth. It was horribly close. Black insects were beginning to buzz in front of his vision. How much longer could he stop himself from screaming, from fighting it off? The guards' hands closed round his wrists and he knew there was no escape. They would not let him defend himself. He could only wait.

With ungainly determination, the huge spider was negotiating more of its legs over the obstacle of Novan's open collar. Clawed tips probed for a foothold on his skin. The pulse pounded in his neck. He felt the first touch of its furred body sac, the closer pressure of living flesh against flesh. He was swaying. He was going to fall.

'*Keep absolutely still.*'

At the same second as Thoughtcatcher's inner cry, there came a flash of light. Cozuman's rod glowed with a vivid orange, horribly outlining the spider as its head lunged towards the hollow in Novan's throat. There was a moment's stillness, in which the orbs of the spider's eyes flamed from black to scarlet. Then it fell away. Novan felt the brush of its hairy sac as it dropped. Eight waving legs found the outstretched pencil of the rod and clung to it. The body hung limp, harmless.

Cozuman carried it back to the box and fastened the lid. He held out his rod in silence and a sorcerer carefully wiped it.

The black dots were dancing more thickly in front of Novan's eyes. Now, surely, he was going to faint.

Cozuman's voice seemed to come to him from the other side of darkness.

'So. It seems you spoke the truth. You cannot control all animals. Either that, or you are outstandingly brave. Hardly likely in a Xerappan, whose people are notorious for running away.'

A far longer body than the spider's stalked out of the shadows. There was the faintest feline growl. Cozuman's eyes widened.

'Ah! The leopard.' He held out his hand. Almond advanced cautiously and allowed him to stroke her head. 'Beautiful. I could almost be tempted to keep one myself, if it didn't mean polluting the purity of Femarrat by employing a Xerappan here.'

Cozuman lifted his gaze to Novan again. 'Remarkable! You were facing a hideous death, and yet your mind could still control this leopard.'

Novan was sure that if he attempted to speak, he would be sick.

'Well? Have you nothing to say?'

'I... She's quite tame, really, sir. And it's late at night...' This time he did bring back the wine and water.

'Yet I understand that leopards in the wild are nocturnal?' Cozuman's voice went on as though nothing had happened.

'We travelled by day to get here, sir. She's very tired.' And so am I, he thought, aching to lie down, to weep, to sleep.

'Still, you interest me. Shall we see your beasts again tomorrow?'

'Mrs Yekhavu wants them to draw the chariot that will take her daughter to the temple on the summit.'

'Does she indeed? Yes, I can imagine that. She thinks I will be impressed.' Then he laughed, low, almost pleasantly. 'Well, perhaps I am.'

Why did Novan shudder?

'Take him back where he belongs,' Cozuman said with abrupt command. 'It will soon be dawn. And watch him carefully tomorrow, if you value your lives. Him and his cats.'

'Her brother Balgo is escorting her to the ceremony, my lord,' the Sorcerer Captain volunteered. 'He's used to handling Xerappans.'

They were outside, and the night was cool enough now to make Novan shiver.

It was a long way down. The steps were steep and treacherous. A new moon had climbed into the sky without Novan noticing it. In its light the staircase shimmered below him, silvery-grey. Several times he stumbled and only the guards kept him from falling. Almond flowed down the steps with liquid grace, though she had climbed them with difficulty.

Novan hardly remembered passing the residence where Alalia was lodged with Mina. She would be sleeping her last night of freedom as Alalia Yekhavu, before she pledged herself to marry Cozuman's nephew. He tried to feel the anger and grief he should have done, but he was too tired.

Only when he paused at the last road, which led to the cat-drivers' hut, did he look back up at the mountain. The sky was beginning to lighten, the stars to fade. Under the crescent moon Mount Femarrat stood out starkly white. Its slopes soared to the mutilated summit, remote, unearthly, streaked with black shadows.

Novan's heart ached. This was his birthright. This mountain had been sacred to the Xerappan people for thousands of years. Yet within his short lifetime they had been pushed out, barred by that Fence. Femarrat belonged to the Children of Yadu now. No Xerappan was allowed to set foot on it.

Except... he shivered with realization. Tomorrow Mina would attend Alalia and he would drive her chariot. They would ascend to that highest sanctuary, where Lord Cozuman would conduct the betrothal ceremony. Once, and once only, he and Mina, two true Xerappans, would stand on the summit of the ancient mountain...

Yet he had to stop this betrothal ceremony from happening.

Chapter Sixteen

Novan could not sleep, desperately tired though he was. He watched the light growing stronger with the merciless advance of a new day. After an hour of restless turning he could stand it no longer. He threw off the thin blanket.

'Get up!' He shook the others. 'We've got the cats to groom and the chariots to get ready. It'll be sunrise soon.'

As if in confirmation, the door of the hut swung open. Two women of the Sorcerer Guard entered, bearing a breakfast of bread rolls and milk.

'Hurry up and eat this. You're wanted at the stables. You'll find everything you need for the betrothal procession is already there. Report to the Yekhavu residence with your vehicles as soon as you're ready. Except for... Which of you is the leopard boy?'

'I am.' Novan stepped forward.

'Emania Yekhavu will ride in the chariot you brought. Harness two of your beasts to it. Someone else will have to drive them. Take your two best animals and bring them separately. Mount Femarrat can provide a more fitting vehicle for the bride-to-be than a Xerappan cart.'

The boys wolfed the food at speed. Even Novan found he was hungry.

When they reached the stables, the alley in front of them seemed full of people. They made their way through the crowd, trying not to bump into uniformed sorcerers.

The space in front of the cliff had been transformed. Where yesterday there had been only black cobbles and white rock, this morning huge baskets of flowers made a riot of colour. The air was heavy with their perfume. Bales of silk spilled out of the harness shed; there were bright heaps of tasselled cushions.

After the first gasp, the boys set to work. There was the spur of pride now as they forced themselves under the slackened Fence wire and began to groom the big cats under the curious stares of the Yadu. The sorcerers waited while the Xerappans cleaned the dirt of travel from the Yekhavus' chariot and the carts which had followed it. Then they moved forward, telling them to drape the vehicles in richly coloured cloth and deck them with flowers, covering even the shafts and the wheel spokes. The festive vehicles made a startling beauty among the lines of barrack huts.

'Here. You'll have to drive Mrs Yekhavu.'

Novan surrendered his chariot to Oniron. He separated out his favourite leopard Almond and her mate Quercus and settled their harness over his arm. Now they were as ready as they could be.

The reality hit him. It was going to happen. All the time he was busy, he could push it to the back of his mind. This was Alalia's betrothal day, when she must solemnly promise to marry Digonez. She had begged him to help her, and he had still done nothing.

Thoughtcatcher was nestled in his sleeve this morning. Novan had changed into the best shirt he had brought. It was more richly embroidered than the one he had travelled in, but there was no second package stitched into the collar. That burden, at least, had been lifted from him. But there was another one that seemed too great to bear.

'What am I going to do?'

'*What I tell you, I hope.*'

118

The procession was moving, mounting the gentle rise to the township he had passed through on his way to Cozuman's house last night. This time they stopped outside a white-walled court, where a jacaranda tree was scattering purple petals. Mina was waiting for them at the gate.

'Bring your leopards in.' She gave him a quick grin, glad to see him, but nervous.

Alalia's ceremonial car was waiting in the cobbled courtyard. The girls had already dressed it in silk and flowers. Hardly any of the original structure showed, but Novan could see that the shafts and wheels were coated with gold. There was no sign of Alalia.

Instead, Balgo stood, immaculate in his white-and-red dress uniform. He was the one still figure among the bustle of preparation, keeping guard over his sister's chariot.

Novan led the two leopards forward and looked at him for permission. Balgo nodded. As he bent to the work of harnessing the cats between the shafts, Novan hoped Balgo would not notice the bulge in his sleeve, where the loose cloth was gathered in at the wrist. He felt the jerboa's tiny paws clinging to his arm.

The lion carts and Oniron's leopard chariot had driven in behind him. Now all Alalia's friends were spilling out of their lodgings, climbing aboard, their brilliant dresses vying with the sheaves of flowers. Emania Yekhavu came out, wearing cloth of gold, under a blue-and-gold parasol. Balgo handed her into Oniron's leopard car.

The procession started to roll out of the gates. The servants who were not accompanying them were cheering and scattering flower petals in front of them.

At last Novan was left alone in the courtyard with Almond and Quercus, meekly waiting with the gilded chariot. Balgo was still vigilant.

The door opened. Alalia came out, with Mina lifting the

train of her skirt above the cobbles.

She was dressed in white, as though this were already her wedding day. It made her pale skin look rosy gold by comparison. A train of silver gauze fell behind from her shoulders, a lace as delicate as the spray from a waterfall. There were lilies in her hand and a circlet of white jasmine in her hair. She looked frail, unearthly, and scared.

Novan lowered his eyes as Balgo handed her into the chariot, but not before he had seen the look she darted at him, a mute appeal for help. So she had not forgotten. Cozuman's spells had not completely wiped from her mind his cruelty last night, or Digonez's. Had the voice of the jerboas, which had recalled Novan and Mina to reality, reached her too? A Child of Yadu, hearing what only Xerappans should?

'*Courage.*'

Novan's eyes shot up in time to see Alalia's startled smile. It was only a moment, then the look of sadness and fear returned. But it left a spark of hope in her eyes.

'You heard Thoughtcatcher again?' His mind reached out for hers.

There was no reply.

He raised the fringed canopy of deep blue and silver, to shade her from the sun.

Mina threw a handful of rose petals over Alalia and stood back. 'Good luck, miss.'

'No!' Alalia seemed to wake out of a trance. 'You've got to come with me, Mina. Tell her, Balgo.'

'Your maid? To the High Sanctuary? Don't be stupid.'

'I need her. What if my dress gets caught on the chariot? Or the wind up there spoils my hair?'

'Oh, women! You're growing as bad as Ma. Well, I suppose she can run behind. As long as she keeps up. I'm not waiting for her.'

With a grin of triumph, Mina ran to seize a bigger basket of flower petals. Almost without Novan thinking about it, Quercus and Almond were starting to ease the chariot forward. The gilded wheels were clattering over the cobbles, releasing fresh waves of perfume from the garlanded spokes. The betrothal car was out on the road and a louder cheer met them. Balgo pointed to his right.

'Up there.'

Novan lifted his eyes. The peak of Mount Femarrat stood clear against the brilliant blue sky. The black temple stood like a scrawl made with charcoal.

'The High Sanctuary. Where the holiest place of our people was, from ancient times,' his mind breathed.

'Don't be ridiculous. On top of everything? That's the Yadu for you. It's what they like to believe. But the truth is utterly different. They've never found our holiest place.'

'Where is it?'

'Just concentrate on your driving, will you? Or none of us will get there.'

The way had been strewn with flowers, already crushed by the procession in front of them. Novan could see it now, winding round the mountain as the slope grew steeper. It was far ahead. Alalia's mother and her attendants would be waiting at the temple by the time the future bride arrived with her brother.

'There's Digonez on his way.'

Novan turned his head to look sideways and up. Another procession had emerged from Cozuman's house, at the head of its green stair. It was following a higher traverse leading to a ridge which would take it straight to the summit. The routes of the two parties were slowly converging.

As the gradient steepened, Almond and Quercus began to strain. The chariot was not large, but leopards are not designed for such work. It was heavy for just two of them to haul it uphill. Novan sang a low encouragement to them. He could hear Thoughtcatcher putting new heart into them, soothing their resentment. Mina toiled behind the chariot, her face hot and sweating, her eyes screwed up against the glare of sun on white rock. Alalia was shaded by the fringed canopy. Balgo wore dark sunglasses.

They came to a point where the road divided. There was no doubt which way Emania Yekhavu and the other girls had gone. The way to the right was scattered with petals, not tossed by well-wishers now, but fallen from the garlands decorating the carts. The road to the left was blank, white, unmarked.

'Left,' ordered Thoughtcatcher.

The leopards were already turning. The warning was only necessary so that Novan would not appear to be steering in the wrong direction. His heart leaped. This was the first step into the unexpected.

'What are you doing?' yelled Balgo. 'Can't you see the road goes right?'

'I have my orders.'

But not from Lord Cozuman.

'Fool! Anyone with half an eye can see which way the others went. Turn round at once.'

Novan could feel, from the prick of heat between his shoulder blades, that the probationer sorcerer's rod was out and trained upon him.

'I'm sorry, sir. I have to do what I'm told.'

'Many ways lead to the sanctuary.'

'There are many ways which lead to the sanctuary,' he repeated aloud.

· *'The left-hand way is the bride's way.'*

'The left-hand way is the bride's way.'

'It's an old Femarrat tradition.'

Was that a hiccup of nervous laughter from Mina, quickly choked off?

The leopards were carrying the flower-decked chariot further and further left, round the shoulder of the mountain.

Alalia said soothingly, 'After all, Balgo, how would you know the paths? You've never been this high up Mount Femarrat, have you? You told me yourself, when you were training here probationers weren't allowed higher than the township. You hadn't even been to Cozuman's house until last night.'

'I don't like it. We've lost sight of the others. What if this idiot gets us lost? A fine set of fools we'd look if you didn't turn up for your betrothal.'

'If only,' murmured Alalia softly.

'*What* did you say?'

Novan could hardly prevent himself from twisting round to look at her. There was a moment's silence, while the wheels juddered over bare rock.

'Balgo... I hate him. Digonez. Two years ago when I first met him, I thought he was wonderfully romantic. But he's growing like his uncle. He's cruel. I'm desperately scared of what it will be like when I'm married and have to live with him.'

'Shut up!'

Novan did turn round then, afraid that the sorcerer was going to strike his sister. Balgo looked furious. He snapped away his spell-rod, as though he realized how close he had come to harming Alalia with it.

'Don't ever say that again.' His voice was low, intense. He glanced around fearfully, as though there might be sorcerers listening on the glittering, bare slopes.

Still the leopards were pacing on, towards a bridge over a shadowed chasm.

'Digonez is Cozuman's nephew,' Balgo hissed at her. 'If you

criticize him, you're criticizing Lord Cozuman.'

'Well? You were there last night. You saw what he did to me. The way he made fun of me, terrified me. And on the night before my betrothal, too. I thought he'd treat me like the guest of honour.'

Novan's eyes were on the bridge ahead now, but he heard the doubt creep into Balgo's voice.

'He only did beautiful things for you. The swans that rained down rubies. The sea of poppies. The river of gold.'

'And the witch who pulled my hair? The elephants that trumpeted fire at me? Those horrible red goblins who picked me up and carried me back to Digonez? Don't forget them.'

'But how can you know that? You're not a sorcerer,' Balgo said slowly. 'You weren't supposed to remember any of that.'

'Oh, wasn't I? It happened, though, didn't it? You've just admitted it. Lord Cozuman scared me out of my wits and then made me look ridiculous. And Digonez was laughing.'

'Cozuman's the High Sorcerer. That's his way. People like us can't expect to understand why he does things. He knows what's best for us. We have to trust him, Alalia. He's the only thing that stands between us and extermination. If it weren't for him, the Xerappans would murder us in our beds and take over our land.'

Take back our land, thought Novan, but dared not say it.

'Then you won't help me? You're a sorcerer. You've got your spell-rod. I... I don't think I can escape from Femarrat without your help.'

'Escape? You mean you're serious? You'd refuse to marry Digonez? Disobey Lord Cozuman?'

'Help me, Balgo, please!'

'Never! What's more, I'm going to warn Digonez to keep a close eye on you from now on. Driver! Stop the car.'

The leopards came to a submissive halt. They were just at the beginning of the bridge. They were out of sight now of the other two processions. They had climbed so much closer to the summit of the mountain that it was hidden by an overhanging ridge. Novan stared down into the chasm that plunged beneath the bridge. At first he thought that the darkness in it was deep shadow, then that it was black scree, like the cobbles of the barrack paths. Now, as his eyes adjusted after the bare white slopes, he began to see that the gorge was tangled with the dark foliage of conifer trees and glossy-leaved bushes. If he had been wearing Balgo's sunglasses it would have looked impenetrably black.

'Turn the chariot round.'

'Balgo! Please!'

'Is this Xerappan in league with you? By the High Sanctuary, I'll strike him dead if he is.'

'Novan has nothing to do with this.'

'*Novan*, is it?'

'We all have names.'

Mina had strolled to the front of the chariot, as though the argument were nothing to do with her. Novan had been aware with some fraction of his mind of scrabbling whispers passing between her and her jerboa. He had far more frightening things to occupy him.

He saw his sister stroke Almond's hindquarters, then move round to Quercus's head. There was something in her hand. A flat white stone from the road, flint-sharp. She leaned over Quercus, crooning in his ears. Her hand moved swiftly, once, twice.

The harness parted. Novan no longer heard what Balgo was shouting at Alalia. For a moment, Quercus looked startled. Then he twitched with the pleasure of feeling himself free. With a smooth bound, his gold-and-black body flew over the side of the bridge and dived into the shelter of the bushes.

'What...' Balgo leaped out of the chariot and ran to the lip of the chasm on his right. His spell-rod was in his hand. There was a flash of red. A pine tree went up in flames.

'*Now! Left!*' The jerboa's command pierced their minds.

Novan and Alalia landed on the other side of the chariot at the same moment. Mina had already cut Almond free too. Before Balgo could turn and see them, they threw themselves down the side of the ravine, rocks slipping under their feet, twigs clawing as they slithered past, the bridge above them now, hiding them from the road.

'*Keep going,*' urged Thoughtcatcher. '*There!*'

As Balgo's shout of fury echoed around the canyon, they found themselves rushing headlong towards a cedar tree. The base of its trunk was split, its roots splayed like giant feet.

'*Down!*'

There was a hole in the soft, resin-scented earth beneath the trunk. A huge, deep hole into utter darkness.

Chapter Seventeen

Alalia hardly hesitated. She grabbed a tree root to steady herself and threw herself over the edge. Her white dress swooped down into the gloom, like an owl flitting into a dark wood. Her voice came muffled, distant.

'It's not too bad. The ground slopes... Ow!'

Almond had leaped after her. There was a scuffle of falling. The white dress disappeared.

Mina shot an anxious look at Novan and swung herself after them.

Novan waited only a moment longer. As he grasped the root, there was a crashing in the woods above him. Balgo's angry shouts came louder. Surely he must see their trail of scuffed earth and broken twigs? But the noise seemed to be moving away from the bridge. Novan was gathering his muscles to follow Mina when his eye was caught by something else. On the slope some way above them a rag of white fluttered from a rhododendron bush. It had been ripped from Alalia's dress as she rushed past. Was there time to go back and remove it? Could he risk Balgo seeing him? But even as he wondered, his foot had already launched him over the edge. He was dropping after Mina. It was too late.

The descent into darkness was an enormous relief. When he landed, the circle of grey light was far above them. It looked no bigger than a coin. Alalia was right about the slope. He was still tumbling down a bank of earth. Soon it became firmer, slightly sticky clay. Pale streaks began to gleam among it. Novan became aware the darkness was not as total as he might have expected. Two faint green beams were lighting the way ahead.

'Novan!' came Mina's astonished cry. 'Look at Almond. Her eyes!'

Novan felt the hair prickle on the back of his neck. 'They're giving out light... They can't! She's never done this before in the dark. We'd have seen it.'

Mina swung round, her curly head silhouetted against the luminous glow. 'She's never been inside Mount Femarrat before.'

'It's *that* sacred?' He looked beyond her in awe, where the rock was tinged with emerald.

The gleam of green showed them the gradient was levelling out. Thoughtcatcher wriggled out of his sleeve and jumped from his wrist to the ground. It was a disappointment to feel the loss of his furry body.

'Is this a tunnel?' Novan spoke low, but the sound of his voice struck him as shockingly dangerous. He glanced behind him and up. The entrance to the hole was no more than a misty star. As he watched, it was blacked out. An avalanche of stones and loose earth came rushing down towards them.

'Balgo must have found us! Run!'

They started to race riskily over the surface they could hardly see.

'*Wait!*' yelled Thoughtcatcher.

They turned. A second, golden, light was bearing down on the jerboa, who sat upright on his long hind legs, facing the newcomer with his ears twitching. Beyond him, they could see nothing but blackness and two brilliant yellow eyes.

'Quercus!' screamed Mina joyfully. 'It's not Balgo at all. We forgot about him. Clever boy!'

The he-leopard paused only momentarily to rub noses with

Thoughtcatcher's tiny one, then he was past them and leaping upon Almond. The two of them rolled on the cave floor, playfully welcoming. The criss-crossing beams of their eyes, green and golden, made a kaleidoscope of the coloured quartz and crystal in the roof and walls. They lit up a tunnel, low-roofed but spacious. The floor was hardening into rock, ridged like the sand when the tide has receded. Whisper had hopped ahead. The lighter patches of her black-and-white fur were coloured by the leopards' eyes.

'Where does it go?' asked Alalia.

Thoughtcatcher was silent for a moment. '*Out,*' he said. '*Or in.*'

The three humans stared down at him, waiting for an explanation. They got none.

'Well,' said Alalia after a while, 'Balgo's back there and, worse, Digonez. I'm going on.'

They began to hurry now, the leopards loping beside them. The jerboas travelled in huge leaps, catapulted forward by their springy hind legs.

They came to a parting of the ways. A wider path went right, a narrower tunnel left.

'Which way?' Alalia was in the lead. She turned to look down at Thoughtcatcher.

'*That depends what you're looking for.*'

'Such as?' They all found it hard not to be impatient.

'*To your right lies the sea. The left-hand way leads into the heart of Mount Femarrat.*'

Alalia immediately began to run to the right. Novan and Mina were close behind her. The slap of their feet on the rock sounded unnaturally loud. The walls echoed with the noise of their laboured breathing.

'The light's getting stronger,' Mina panted. 'It's not just Quercus and Almond's eyes, is it?'

They rounded a bend, and daylight flooded the ridged rock

129

floor in front of them. Caught in the sunshine, they glimpsed tamarisk bushes, a golden beach, a turquoise sea.

Alalia moaned.

Across the perfect semicircle of the tunnel mouth, between them and the beach, was the silver lattice-work of a sorcerers' Fence.

Alalia leaned against the rock wall, breathing heavily, as though her legs would no longer support her. There were tears in her eyes. 'We're trapped.'

Novan looked back over his shoulder. 'There was that other tunnel.'

'That one goes deeper in. Thoughtcatcher told us.'

'It looks like our only way.'

He began, reluctantly, to walk back into the shadow. Mina hesitated, then followed him. For several moments Alalia stayed where she was, staring longingly at the vision of sunshine and freedom she could not reach. Then she pulled herself away from the wall and straggled after them.

The sound of their feet was slower now.

The noise in the tunnel grew louder. Waves of sound were rolling towards them, overtaking and passing them, echoing back from the walls behind them. The fugitives clutched each other, questioning with frightened eyes. Now there were pounding footsteps coming, the clatter of harder heels, a voice shouting, when they could disentangle the echoes, 'Stop there! Or I'll spell-strike you!'

'Balgo!' Alalia was poised on one foot, as though desperately unsure whether to turn and flee, or stand.

Mina shrieked and started to run back, but Novan grabbed her.

'Don't be a fool! He's got his sorcerer's rod.'

The racing strides came on. In the same instant, Thoughtcatcher and Whisper leaped back to hide in the folds of the Xerappans' clothing.

'It sounds as if he's still on his own,' breathed Alalia. 'But he's a sorcerer. He'll take me back to Digonez! What can we *do*?'

Novan begged Thoughtcatcher for an answer, but no wisdom came.

Balgo filled the height of the tunnel. The boots of his uniform rattled on the rock. His spell-rod was in his hand, dangerously advanced towards them. It was flashing with red fire. The leopards flattened their ears. The green and gold light from their eyes made his flushed face more lurid.

Alalia stepped forward to meet him. She was breathing fast. 'It was my idea. I had to get away from Digonez. These two Xerappans are my servants. I ordered them to follow me. You can't blame them.'

Balgo was watching the leopards. They sank down on their bellies and rolled over, harmless as kittens. He allowed his glance to shift to Novan. 'I'm glad you're being sensible. You know what will happen if those brutes make one threatening move.'

'Understood, sir.'

'I'm taking you back,' the young sorcerer snapped at his sister. 'Whether Digonez will still want to marry you after this, I very much doubt. As well as disgracing our family, you've humiliated him and, worst of all, insulted Lord Cozuman. He'll certainly make you pay for that.'

'And you don't care? Your job's worth more than my happiness?'

'Of course I care! I care about the dignity of Femarrat, about the honour of our family, about the freedom of the land of Yadu, and everything we've built here. How could you damage that? I'm ashamed you're my sister.'

'The freedom of Yadu? And for that, you'd force your own sister to marry against her will, to a man you know to be

131

cruel? What kind of freedom is that?'

'We all make sacrifices for our country.'

'Does that include sacrificing the Xerappans? What about Sea Pines? A whole village slaughtered by sorcerers?'

'That didn't happen,' Balgo ground through clenched teeth. 'It's a Xerappan lie.'

'So the Xerappans just ran away at the sight of us? We never did anything to terrify them into fleeing for the hills?'

'They've got their own land there. We need ours.'

'So why are we planting colonies on their hills, too? Across the border Fence. Balgo, we *live* there!'

'Only for security. If we didn't control the Xerappans, they'd start a war against us.'

'Wouldn't you, if you were a Xerappan?'

'Where did you learn that kind of talk? I'm Yadu, thank the stars.'

'So the Children of Yadu have rights, but Xerappans don't?'

He stared at her. 'You're beginning to sound like one of them.' His eyes darted to Novan and Mina. 'Is this some kind of sorcery? Have you put a spell on her, like you do on the leopards...?' His voice trailed off. He was staring at the glow from the big cats' faces. 'Their eyes! Did you do *that*? If you've bewitched my sister...'

'No, sir.' Novan shook his head. 'I couldn't control her mind, even if I wanted to. It doesn't work on humans.'

'So you say.'

'It's my fault,' Mina said in a small voice. 'I told her about our family. About Father and Mother having to pick up Novan when he was a baby, and run for their lives in the middle of the night. About the Sorcerer Guard setting fire to their orange groves, in their farm by the sea. About how Grandmother still has the key to her house, but the Yadu will never let her go home.'

Balgo was breathing quickly, trying to shut his ears to what

132

they were saying. 'You're still children. You don't understand. Lord Cozuman knows what's necessary, better than any of us.'

'Does he know the power of love?'

A flame leaped in Alalia's eyes. Her head turned, as if to check where the thought was coming from.

Balgo shook his head, as though something had confused him too.

Can it be, Novan thought wonderingly, that *he* almost heard?

The rod of power glowed less fiercely, faltered in Balgo's hand. But Novan was terrified that any moment the sorcerer would recollect his duty and force them to the headquarters of the Sorcerer Guard.

'You can choose, sir. There's a Fence behind us. On the other side is a beach. If you love your sister, you could open that Fence and let her go. We'd help her find a boat and escape beyond Yadu. I'll look after her.'

Balgo seemed to be struggling for breath.

'Bal...' Alalia started to plead, then closed her lips. They were in his hands.

The young sorcerer looked over their heads, then behind him. He tapped his spell-rod against his palm. He licked his lips.

'Do you love her?'

Balgo's eyes widened. The corners of his lips twitched nervously.

'It's a little late for your betrothal ceremony and, anyway, that dress is ruined. But if Lord Cozuman even suspected I helped you...' He shuddered. None of them dared to breathe. 'Well, suppose I plead the leopards sprang on me and you escaped? But I'll still be court-martialled. He'll say I should have killed the leopards, and you too, sister or not.' He was plainly frightened.

Alalia threw herself on her brother's neck and kissed him.

'But you'll help us? Oh, thank you! I knew it! I couldn't believe they'd taken you over completely. Though after a year's training with the Sorcerer Guard, it was a close thing.'

'Don't push your luck. I still *am* a sorcerer, remember. Shut up and get moving. But I don't think this is going to work.'

Balgo watched the leopards rise either side of him with renewed anxiety. They pressed towards the daylight, with Mina in the lead.

Light flooded the tunnel. The sand sparkled through the lattice in the Fence. Balgo took his sunglasses from his pocket, as if wondering whether to put them on again.

Alalia shot an alarmed look at her brother. 'You can open it, can't you? You've got your rod.'

Balgo licked his lips. His spell-rod was out, but glowing only faintly. 'I'm still a probationer. And that's a powerful Fence.'

'Does it mean the sorcerers know about these tunnels?' Novan looked anxiously back into the darkness.

'Mount Femarrat is our headquarters. Of course we know everything about it. Or Lord Cozuman does.'

'*Does he really?*'

Again, that slight shock passed across Balgo's face.

'Go on, then,' begged Alalia. 'Open it. Hurry.'

'There's bound to be a boat somewhere, isn't there?' Mina was edging as close to the Fence as she dared, trying to peer through. 'Even if we have to steal it.'

The light of the spell-rod was gathering intensity. Balgo was muttering words half under his breath. The other three wanted to cover their ears, sure that they must not hear what he was saying.

The lattice shimmered. It was as though the sky were becoming part of the silvery metal. It was hard to see whether it parted or dissolved. But the sand was searingly bright, the water brilliant. There was nothing between them and freedom but the last few steps of the tunnel.

They looked at each other, all four humans afraid. The leopards were first, gliding forward into the open, their green and golden eyes fading in the fiercer brilliance of the beach. The others followed. The fugitives shuddered in spite of themselves as they passed between the jagged wings of the Fence.

They were out, and the sand was burning under sandalled feet.

'I have to close that Fence.' Balgo stopped. 'If a breach is left open for more than a minute or two, alarms will sound in Headquarters.'

'Hurry, then.' Alalia and the Xerappans were looking nervously round the sheltered cove. They could see only embracing arms of black rock and the dancing sea ahead.

Balgo raised his rod and pointed it back at the tunnel mouth. It glowed warmly golden. A frown creased his forehead. He lifted his left hand to join his right. He seemed to be straining every muscle. The others waited in silence, glancing occasionally over their shoulders.

The Fence began to move. Balgo let out a sigh. Then he gripped his rod tighter. Terrible words were forced through his lips. The gap through the mesh remained, a black void separating the halves of silver.

'I can't... do... it!' The words, in normal Yaduan speech, groaned through his lips. 'It won't... close.'

The leopards growled.

Far across the mountain, unearthly howls shook the sky, scattering screeching flocks of parakeets. Flashes of light, more brilliant than the sun and far closer, streaked above the cove, hitting the sea in explosions of foam.

'They know we're here!' Alalia screamed.

'I warned you,' shouted Balgo. 'Cozuman knows

135

everything.'

'Look!' Mina's voice rose out of control. She pointed a shaking finger. 'What *is* it?'

Where the flash of the spells had struck the sea, a darker life was writhing upwards. It was as though black whip thongs were lashing the waves. Through mounting spray those racing loops swooped and rose, cutting a glittering way straight to the beach.

'Sea serpents!' yelled Balgo. 'Get back in the tunnel!'

Novan grabbed Alalia's hand. 'I'm sorry! I really thought we'd done it.'

'Not your fault.' She tried to smile, though her face was pale. 'Now shut up and run.'

For a terrifying moment, they thought the Fence would leap to close as they rushed between its parted teeth. But they were through, though feeling the shock of its force from head to toe. They plunged from brilliance back into darkness.

'The Guard will find us soon,' panted Balgo. 'We'd be better surrendering. You don't know how they can blast these tunnels.' But he was still running.

'Not thinking of giving up already, are you?' came Thoughtcatcher's voice. *'After all, you haven't tried everything, have you?'*

Chapter Eighteen

They came to the junction of the tunnels. One way led back to the deep hole under the cedar. The other was narrower, darker. The white rock changed to black.

Novan did not need to ask Thoughtcatcher. 'They'll expect us to try to get out, not in.'

'But we've got to get out in the end. How *will* we?' Mina's voice was rising.

'Anything, so long as Digonez doesn't capture me.' For Alalia, another fear was uppermost.

'I'm going on.' Novan moved forward. 'Didn't you hear Thoughtcatcher? We haven't tried everything.'

There was a gasp. Mina and Alalia were staring at Novan, then at Balgo, with barely disguised dismay. The young sorcerer's face looked puzzled in the spell-light.

'Heard who? I thought a voice I didn't recognize said something like that. Who's Thoughtcatcher?'

Before he could stop it, there was a squirming in Novan's sleeve. Thoughtcatcher emerged, sat on his hand, and started combing his whiskers with his tiny front paws. His large round eyes studied the probationer sorcerer.

'*I'm Thoughtcatcher.*'

'*And I'm Whisper.*' The black-and-white jerboa ran up on to Mina's shoulder.

Novan's nerves screamed silently, Why didn't I keep my mouth shut? If Balgo betrays us now, the whole Sorcerer

137

Guard will know about the jerboas. Cozuman will know. All the Children of Yadu will know. We'll have lost our only advantage.

And then: Does this mean I have to kill Balgo, now?

Balgo gazed at the jerboas with a strange expression. 'You?' He reached out a finger and touched Thoughtcatcher's ear. 'Little things like you can...?' He looked suddenly up into Novan's eyes. 'Is that how you do it? This mouse-thing? If it can speak in my mind, does it speak to leopards? Not just speak, but control them?'

Novan nodded.

'It wasn't you doing it, at all?'

'No.'

Balgo allowed his stare to travel sideways over Almond and Quercus. 'So it's as well to be polite to jerboas.' He managed an uncertain smile.

'You've got your spell-rod,' Alalia pointed out. 'You could blast them dead. The leopards, the jerboas. If you wanted to.'

For answer, Balgo started to slip his rod into the sheath on his belt, but the light in the tunnel faded rapidly and he drew it out again.

'We're wasting time.'

The leopards leaped ahead, the eerier beams of their eyes reaching beyond the pool of light which Balgo directed at the feet of the hurrying humans. This tunnel shelved deeper.

'Where is it taking us?' whispered Alalia.

Novan checked. 'Listen!'

They all halted before a dip in the floor, beyond which the way rose again. There was water in the hollow below them, reflecting the glow of Balgo's rod. The green and gold leopard-light played over rough rocks on either side.

Far away, distorted by distance, they heard other noises in the tunnel.

Balgo twisted his rod across his hand, studying it intently

at each position.

'We're close to the centre of the mountain. This tunnel slopes up to Cozuman's house.'

'Is that where those sounds are coming from?' Alalia clutched his arm.

Thoughtcatcher leaped from Novan's wrist. There was a tiny splash as he hit a puddle. Then he was off, hardly discernible among the black stones. Presently there was a scamper of sound, a scrabbling of tiny claws on rock.

'He's climbing the wall,' whispered Mina, as the leopards swung round to watch.

The ominous sounds were coming nearer. Men's voices were clearly distinguishable now.

'What can we do?' breathed Alalia. 'What if it's Digonez?'

'Follow Thoughtcatcher.'

Novan splashed into the hollow. The leopards were already swarming up the rock, gripping crevices with their claws. It was harder for human hands and feet. Novan hoisted Mina as high as he could, while Balgo helped Alalia up. The girls climbed further.

'There's a ledge here,' hissed Mina. 'It goes a long way back.'

Novan scrambled up to it.

Balgo swung his first foot off the ground, then he stopped. He dropped back into the shallow water. The leopards closed their eyes so that no light showed from them.

'Balgo!' urged Alalia. 'Quick!' Her white dress had sunk into the shadows.

The oncoming noises were magnified in the tunnel. It sounded like an army advancing.

Balgo stood his ground, facing them.

'Is he going to betray us?' gasped Mina.

'Go, before the sorcerers' rods sense you.'

Novan and Mina were used to obeying their jerboas' orders

without question. They retreated rapidly to the back of the ledge. Their hands felt an edge of rock, and then space. Still trusting, they let themselves drop over. Novan was just about to let go when he realized that Alalia was not following them. He cursed under his breath. Either her mind was not yet sufficiently tuned to the jerboas' messages, or she did not understand that instant obedience could be a matter of life or death.

Shouts were echoing round the cavern, making it sound as though guards were advancing from all directions. They had seen Balgo.

'Balgo... algo... algo!' the walls thundered.

The roars smothered Alalia's tiny shriek. Whisper had scampered back and bitten her. She fumbled her way through the darkness to the others, away from the spell-light flooding the tunnel.

'But Balgo's still there. We can't leave him.'

'Don't be an idiot. He meant us to.'

'If Digonez finds Balgo's helping us to escape...' Alalia pleaded, 'can you imagine how he'll punish him?'

'If you don't come off that ledge, he certainly *will* find out. Didn't you hear Thoughtcatcher?'

Novan took one hand from the rock and reached up to grab Alalia's dress. Then he let go with the other, dragging her with him. She fell on top of him in a heap on a stone floor. Fortunately, it was close enough not to hurt him much. One of the leopards rubbed itself against him in the darkness.

They crouched, hoping the thick wall of stone would shield them from the search of sorcerers' rods.

'Balgo Yekhavu! What in the name of a thousand demons are you doing down here? Where's Alalia?' At the sudden loudness of Digonez's shout, Alalia gripped Novan's arm.

'She's escaped...' Balgo's answer was harder to make out.

'Escaped! What do you mean? I was waiting for her on the

mountain top. She was on her way to be betrothed to me!'

'... leopards... found this tunnel... some sort of explosion...'

'Some idiot opened a Fence down by the sea, but couldn't shut it. Set off the protection system. But the guards found no one dead on the beach ... What are you talking about, "*She ran away*?" You were escorting her!'

'Don't blame me! Have you got a sister?'

'Didn't you throw a slay-spell after them? You let them go?'

'By the time I found the tunnel entrance, they were way ahead of me. And the tunnel forks.'

'Thank you, Balgo Yekhavu. I know *exactly* what these tunnels do, a great deal better than you appear to ... What are you waiting for? *March*! And scan the tunnel walls for hiding places as you go. The merest hint of body heat, slam a stun-spell at it. I want to take them alive. When I find that slut, she's going to regret she was ever born.'

Alalia clutched Novan in the darkness. 'He's taking Balgo with him.'

But Digonez's order rapped out. 'And *you*, Probationer Yekhavu, get back to Lord Cozuman's headquarters as fast as you can. You think you can make fools of the High Sorcerer's family? I rather imagine your probationary year is about to end prematurely, and very unpleasantly. Some sorcerer!'

The tramp of boots resounded down the tunnel. It was a long time before silence fell. The smaller glow of Balgo's spell-light went out. They heard his boots scrape as he climbed the rock in the darkness. No one dared to call to him. His clothes rustled over the ledge above them. There was a slight clatter of his sorcerer's rod.

'*Stop,*' Thoughtcatcher's command went out. '*Feel for the edge, then just let yourself go.*'

They moved back, leaving a space for him to drop among them. Almond opened her eyes. A soft green light glimmered on the scene.

Alalia hugged Balgo, unable to speak.

Mina squeezed Novan's hand. 'I was wrong about him.'

Brother and sister looked around them curiously. The two jerboas sat up on their haunches and groomed their whiskers. A new tunnel stretched out in front of them. Its floor became sandier. Fragments of quartz shone like emeralds in the leopard-light. The roof was arched.

'It's funny,' said Mina. 'It's sort of peaceful here. Not so threatening as that other tunnel.'

'It's just the relief,' said Alalia, turning. 'If we hadn't got here just as Digonez came... If Thoughtcatcher hadn't climbed the wall... If there hadn't been this cave to hide us...'

The jerboas combed their whiskers faster than before.

'I think,' said Novan quietly, 'it wasn't *all* coincidence.'

'And if Digonez *hadn't* been chasing us,' said Mina, 'we might never have found this cave existed. Do you think it leads somewhere?'

She started forward, the leopards keeping pace with her. Quercus had opened his golden eyes too. The semicircular passage ahead glittered.

'It's going down,' said Alalia presently.

Balgo stopped. He was still shaking. 'I hoped this would be an escape route. I want to get out to the light and the air, not be buried under the mountain.'

'Thoughtcatcher said this leads to the heart of Femarrat.' Novan was feeling nervous too, but he tried not to show it.

'I thought that meant the middle, and then we'd come out on the far side. Not down to the bottom... if there is a bottom. We'll be trapped. Now the alarm's sounded, Cozuman will have strengthened the defences around Femarrat. And they were pretty scary already.'

'There's no other way for us.' Mina's voice trailed back hollowly. 'Digonez's sorcerers are searching the tunnels behind us. But I'm beginning to wonder if they know about this one. He was standing right under the ledge, yet he didn't order them to search it. It feels sort of... clean.'

'What are you suggesting?' There was anger in Balgo's voice. 'That I'm not? Because I'm a sorcerer?'

'Hush, Balgo,' Alalia pacified him. 'Mina's a Xerappan, remember. You can't expect her to *like* sorcerers... in general. But you're different. You saved us all back there. If you'd dropped the slightest hint to Digonez...'

'Yes, Balgo! I'm really, really sorry. I didn't mean *you*.'

It was not until Balgo's hand dropped to his hip that the others realized he had drawn his rod and was pointing it at Mina, his finger poised to throw a felling-spell. He was still a sorcerer.

They went on silently.

'This tunnel's not just going *down*,' called Mina, after a while. 'It's going *round*.'

Even in the dim glow of the leopards' eyes, there could be no mistaking the curve in the passage in front of her.

'We don't know what's round that bend,' muttered Balgo. 'Maybe I should go in front.'

'Thoughtcatcher?' Novan questioned.

'Please yourselves.'

'I think that means it's OK.'

They edged cautiously around the curving wall. There was nothing to be seen but more tunnel.

'The slope's getting steeper.' Mina was going more slowly now, her hands on the leopards each side for reassurance.

They followed it ever downwards, on round a curve that seemed never to end.

'We must have walked round in a circle,' Novan said.

'It's a spiral.' Alalia traced her hand around the walls. 'Because we keep going lower.'

'Do you think it's a maze?' laughed Mina. 'You're supposed to dance through them, aren't you?' She began to skip.

'Don't play the fool!' called Novan, suddenly anxious.

Mina fell back to a more sedate walk. 'It's not that we *shouldn't* dance here. Only it ought to be a more solemn dance, with drums and flowers and the smoke from burning spices.'

'It's just a tunnel,' said Alalia.

'*Is it?*'

The passage was twisting so tightly now that Alalia and Novan could not see the pair in front. They had lost the light from the leopards' eyes. Alalia bumped into the rock and stumbled back to clutch Novan.

'Wait!' he called to the others. 'We can't see.'

Balgo hissed a few words. The answer was a shocking flare of light as his sorcerer's rod shot a beam of white, just tinged with red, along the passage towards them. Though they could not see him, the spell-light illuminated the rock wall around which he had just disappeared.

'Put it out!' Mina and Novan both cried.

'You were complaining you couldn't see.'

'It's...' Mina struggled to find the words. 'It's just that this isn't that sort of place. Can't you feel it? I thought Lord Cozuman knew everything. But I don't believe he's ever been here.'

'You can't tell that,' Alalia objected.

Balgo let the beam of his rod linger over the walls just a little longer. Then he snapped it off. 'She's right. This is new. It's never been explored before.'

'*You mean, by sorcerers.*'

'Well, yes. That's what my rod's telling me.'

'*And can your spell-rod tell you who was here, once?*' teased Thoughtcatcher.

'No.'

There was a gasp from Mina ahead.

'What's wrong?' Novan tried to push to the front.

'Nothing's... wrong.' Her voice trailed slowly up to them. 'At least... Somebody *has* been here before us ... You've got to see this!'

Chapter Nineteen

They followed her voice down the last twisting bend, almost stumbling over each other in their haste. The tunnel opened suddenly into a low-roofed chamber. In the dim green and gold of the leopards' eyes, it was impossible to guess how wide it was. The narrow beams played here and there over the walls, illuminating first one small area, then another.

The humans gasped.

Everywhere they looked, the rock had been painted. The cavern might have been hung with tapestries.

'It's just like you said, Mina! The dancing!' Alalia's voice was hushed with awe.

As Quercus and Almond's eyes travelled along the wall, they followed a procession of dancers. There were young men and women with wreaths of flowers round their heads, their necks, their arms. Hands met as they circled, feet leaped, hair swung. Blue smoke eddied among them from incense burners swinging on silver chains. Musicians with drums and horns and lyres led the procession.

'Look at the land!' cried Novan.

Beyond the dancers lay the sea, turquoise under a sapphire sky. Fishermen hauled in their nets. The fields stood rich with corn and fruiting palms. Women were carrying full baskets of vegetables. Cows spurted milk generously into pails. In the distance, camels swung across the desert, laden with goods.

'Xerappo!' breathed Novan. 'This is what it used to be like.'

'It's not,' Balgo snapped. 'It's the plain of Yadu.'

'Look at the people! Their black hair, everything. They're just like us.'

'Before we invaded you,' murmured Alalia.

Mina moved along the wall. Almond moved with her. Her green beams parted from Quercus's gold, making the deeper recesses of the cavern more mysterious. For the others, the land glowed even more joyful in the light of Quercus's gold eyes alone.

'Novan!' Mina's sudden cry came from the further end of the cavern. As they spun round, they saw the phosphorescent green from Almond's eyes travelling in a huge arc, whose end was still lost in darkness.

'Alalia! Quick! You must see this!'

They hurried to join her. The light skitter of paws told of the jerboas leaping alongside them. Quercus raised his eyes to illuminate more brightly the painted panel which faced the entrance to this cavern.

'This must be where the procession is going!' Novan's voice was rising in excitement.

This scene was even more magnificent than the dancing procession and the harvest fields. A host of people knelt. Their colourful robes spread around them in a wide semicircle. These were not just Xerappans. Their hair, their skin, their faces, their build, proclaimed them to come from many nations. Their hands offered up gifts, gold and silver, carved ebony, sandalwood boxes, strings of jewels, peacock fans.

The watchers saw where all their outstretched hands were reaching, and gasped. Painted so large they dwarfed this multitude, two people sat on resplendent thrones. One was a man, the other a woman. Rich vestments, crusted with embroidery, glittering with gems, draped them from shoulders to feet. Round their head both wore a circlet of

147

gold leaves. The left hand of the man held a crystal sphere, girdled with rubies. In the right hand of the woman was a rod of silver. On the shoulder of each of them, a jerboa perched. The man's was grey-brown, like Thoughtcatcher, the woman's a more exotic patchwork of yellow and white. The jerboas' four round black eyes stared out of the picture and held theirs.

But what had drawn that gasp from the two Xerappans and the two Children of Yadu gazing at them were the faces and hair of the man and woman on the thrones. The man was the shorter of the two, with blunt features and curling black hair. A true Xerappan, like Novan. The woman was tall, with a slender face and long, straight hair, fair as the stalks of wheat. Just like Alalia.

'A Child of Yadu.' Alalia whispered what they could all see. 'A queen in Xerappo?'

'When a Xerappan was king?' Novan turned to look at her. Their eyes held each other's.

'Nobody told us. My people certainly didn't.'

Novan shook his head. 'Mine neither. It's always been "us" and "them".'

'Then... if we weren't always separate...'

'Some Xerappans must still be partly Yadu? And the other way round?'

Their hands were reaching out towards each other.

A shout roared down the spiral tunnel. The distorted sounds made no sense, but the four in the cavern did not need to be told who was coming.

'Digonez! He's found the passage!'

'Is there a way out at the other end?' Novan started to run towards the darkness.

'No,' moaned Mina. 'I've already looked.'

'What about *there*?' Startlingly, Balgo switched the light of his spell-rod to the centre of the picture.

'Put it out! He'll see us!' Alalia gasped.

The light quivered. Balgo, who was as frightened as any of them, was having difficulty holding his arm steady. 'Weren't any of you listening to Thoughtcatcher?'

Novan's mouth fell open. Could this Yadu sorcerer really have heard Thoughtcatcher, when *he* had not?

The jerboa's black eyes glinted up at them. He seemed to be smiling.

'Look!'

Balgo's trembling spell-light brought to life the centre of the picture, between the two thrones and the semicircle of kneeling figures. They had all assumed this was a blue-green carpet. But as the light focused on it, they saw that bubbles rose and danced on its surface. A faint vapour, which could not be incense smoke, breathed from it. It was a circular pool of water.

'Alalia! I know you're down there! Damn you, Balgo, for a traitor!' The walls menaced them with a multiplication of Digonez's yells.

Balgo swung round and the leopards' eyes followed his light.

The pool was not just in the painting. It was here, in the centre of the cavern which had once been the throne room at the heart of Mount Femarrat. As Balgo switched off his spell-rod, the water glistened more green than blue in the leopard-light. Mist wreathed from it.

'The pool!' Mina exclaimed. 'Don't you remember? When Grandfather married Grandmother on Mount Femarrat, they dressed her in a yellow wig like a Yadu woman. This must be why. And then the Guardian led them down into a pool. '

She ran to the edge and peered over. Green and gold bubbles rose to meet her, like winking eyes.

'What good is that?' Novan could hardly stop himself shouting. 'We need a way *out*. Fast!'

'I think the way is here,' said Balgo in a low voice. 'But I don't understand how.'

'Do it!' Mina stamped her foot. 'Novan, you want to marry Alalia one day, don't you? And she wants to get betrothed to you, not Digonez. Quick! Take her hand. Let's all get into the pool.'

'Now?'

'You can do this, can't you?' she rounded on Balgo. 'You're a sorcerer.'

'I... it was going to be Lord Cozuman who betrothed them. I'm only a probationer.'

'WE'VE GOT YOU NOW, LIKE RATS IN A HOLE!'

The rod shook in Balgo's hand. His face was white as he stared at the tunnel down which Digonez's voice was booming.

Novan turned to look at Alalia. 'Will you?'

Her eyes were huge with fear and excitement. '*Yes!* If it's the last thing I do.'

Their hands clasped as they splashed into the pool together. Balgo was wading into the blue-green water too, with Mina beside him.

The yells and the march of boots were almost upon them.

'I don't know the right words. What would your Guardian have said?'

'Just *do* it!' urged Mina, almost beside herself. She scooped up handfuls of water and threw them over her brother and Alalia.

Balgo turned to face them. 'Do you two love each other more than anyone in the world?'

'We do!'

More showers flashed like jewels in the leopards' eyes.

The fierce light of spell-rods had reached the lower end of the tunnel.

'Will you be loyal to each other as long as you live?' Balgo forced the words out.

'We will!'

Noise thundered around them. 'SAY YOUR PRAYERS, ALALIA YEKHAVU, AND ANYONE WITH YOU!'

Balgo turned in dread. It was Mina's clear voice which rose above the echoes. 'Will you serve the land and the people of Yadu and Xerappo, in truth and peace and justice?'

'We will.'

'As long as we live!' gasped Alalia.

The water cascaded over all of them.

'TRY AND TRICK ME THIS TIME, AND I'LL GRIND YOU VERY SLOWLY TO PEPPER DUST AND BURNING ASHES!'

Novan and Alalia threw their arms round each other.

'He can, too,' muttered Balgo. 'I've seen what they do to prisoners.'

'We've heard,' said Novan.

'What can we do?' begged Alalia.

'The pool! Can't you feel it?' cried Mina, who was standing deeper in the water than any of them. 'It wants to pull us down. Just like Grandfather said! Come on!'

The first blast of spell-strike seared across the cavern, deflected by the final twist of the tunnel round which Digonez was coming. Ancient pictures shattered, ricocheting off the floor in jewel-bright fragments.

'Drown ourselves?' protested Novan. 'To spite Digonez?'

'If he catches you alive, you'll wish you had,' muttered Balgo.

'*Stop arguing, you idiots,*' Thoughtcatcher rapped. '*Jump!*'

From the edge of the pool, both jerboas sprang. Two tiny plops and they were gone.

Mina dived head first. There was a moment's hesitation, then Balgo disappeared in a cloud of spray.

Alalia's eyes were wide with alarm. Novan's hand held hers. For a moment they smiled at each other. Then they plunged.

151

Novan was aware of Alalia falling beside him, feet first, like him. Her long fair hair streamed upwards, like the shimmering stems of waterweed. Silver bubbles rose through green water, which was growing ominously brighter. The Sorcerer Guard was in the throne room above them.

We're still dropping, Novan thought to himself. We'll have to surface soon to breathe. But that means rising back to face Digonez. This can't be a way out.

It was harder to see downwards. A cloud of bubbles obscured Balgo's head below him. Mina was diving like a fish. On either side of her the leopards were plunging as sleekly as otters.

He could hear nothing. But the water suddenly shuddered with explosive force. The distant surface shattered into a brilliant chaos. Novan felt Alalia squeeze his hand. If there had been air, they would have gasped.

The pool was growing darker. As they looked up, huge lumps of rock massed above them, shutting out the light. The boulders were falling, following them down. Big enough to crush them.

Novan's chest was heaving, panting for air. *Panting?* He looked around, bewildered. Where had the bubbles gone? Alalia's hair was settling over her shoulders. Below him, Mina squatted on a sandy floor, scratching Whisper's spoon-like ears.

'*What kept you?*' asked Thoughtcatcher, as they landed beside him.

'I can breathe!' marvelled Alalia. 'We're not in the water. We're *under* it.'

Nothing made sense. The space where they crouched was roofed with water. The bottom of the pool was only just above their heads, darkened now by the slowly tumbling mass of rocks. Novan knew that if he reached up his hand he would touch that cool liquid underbelly. Yet here it was no more than moist. His lungs drew in air, not water.

Mina cuddled Whisper and looked around her with wondering eyes. 'Have we come to the bottom of everything? Is this the heart of the world? Not the room with the paintings, but here, *under* the mountain?'

'Move, you idiots!' snapped Balgo. 'Unless you want to be hit by tons of rock. Digonez is destroying that painted chamber.'

'Those wonderful pictures!' mourned Mina, scrambling away at the same time. 'All our history! Just when we'd discovered it. He can't just wipe out the past, can he?'

'He's the High Sorcerer's nephew. He can do pretty much what he likes.'

The sand shook. Slabs of rock, some painted, some torn raw from the walls behind, crashed where the fugitives had just been crouching. As more hit them, the noise became appalling, until the heap rose so high that the water lapped round its slopes. In the eerie silence which followed, the debris grew so mountainous that it shut out the last light from the sorcerers' rods. They were plunged into a gloom which only the leopards' eyes lit.

'We're trapped here for ever now. There's no way back up,' murmured Alalia.

'There wouldn't have been, anyway,' Balgo said grimly. 'None of us would have dared to go back there.'

'It's like the bottom of a well,' said Mina. 'Only there's no water down here. Well, not much. It must be a very special place.'

'Will we ever get out?' asked Alalia.

It was what they were all wondering.

'Thoughtcatcher said, "*Jump*".' Novan looked at his jerboa almost accusingly.

The jerboa was busy attending to an itch at the base of his tail.

'I felt it.' Balgo fingered his sorcerer's rod. 'When I turned my spell-light on the pool in the picture, the shock seemed to go right through my arm, to my heart. I knew this mattered more than anything.'

Thoughtcatcher's eyes shone up at him, like two black pools themselves.

'I owe you an apology,' Alalia murmured to her brother. 'I really thought you were on Digonez's side. That you didn't understand.'

'I didn't,' he said. 'Not then.'

'I... I think I've found something.' Mina's voice trailed from further away.

They felt their way towards her. Mina's face was in shadow. The leopards were training their eyes beyond her; Quercus's gold beams were slanted to the right, Almond's green ones to the left. They played over two stone sculptures, sitting side by side, staring back at them with round carved eyes.

'Jerboas,' breathed Novan. 'Down here too?'

Mina caught her breath. 'That day Grandfather was telling us about Mount Femarrat, what name did Thoughtcatcher give it?'

'The Jerboas' Nest.'

Neither of the little creatures would catch their eye. They were gazing at the shadows between the statues with a still intensity.

'Is that a doorway?' Balgo bent his head to peer into the darkness.

'If it is, it's very small,' said Mina.

'It might be the way out!' There was a sudden rise of hope in Alalia's voice.

'*Or the way in?*' Thoughtcatcher had been silent for so long that the question made them all jump.

'Into what?' demanded Novan.

He waited. Balgo and Alalia looked at the Xerappans

154

questioningly, wondering if their inexperienced minds had failed to hear something. Thoughtcatcher, as so often, gave no answer.

'I think,' Novan explained, 'he means there's only one way to find out.'

Chapter Twenty

'It's very low,' Mina pointed out. 'Even for me. I'd have to go down on my hands and knees.'

Novan did just that. The others followed. They were becoming like jerboas themselves, creeping into some secret place. Now the stone jerboas rose taller than them.

The sand here was dry under Novan's hands; it felt warmer. As he approached the opening, he had to bend his neck still lower. As he put his head under the arch of rock, he sensed a thrill of wonder. Twice he had thought he had reached the heart of Femarrat, the sacred mountain. First the painted throne room, then the underneath of the pool. Now, this low doorway into mystery. It was plain, small, dark. He shuffled forward on his knees.

His groping hands came to rest on softness. His fingertips explored yielding fibres. Grass, tufts of hair, even tiny, curling feathers. It felt like a nest.

The disturbance he made released a wave of scent. After ages of journeying through rock and sand and water, he breathed hay, the far-off memory of a meadow of summer flowers, and something warmer, animal.

He stayed very still, wondering who might be in such a nest. The silence lengthened. A tiny part of his mind was aware of the impatience of the others behind him, but that seemed unimportant now. If he moved at all into this hollow, it must be slowly, quietly, with reverence.

He could hear nothing except the tiny sigh of his own breath. Yet he felt a presence filling the darkness. It brought a wave of tiredness sweeping over him, tears stinging his eyes. He was a little boy again, comforted in his parent's arms. After all that had happened to him, he could rest here. He would be looked after, loved.

'*Novan!*' Mina was shaking his ankle.

Reluctantly, Novan staggered to his feet. He put out his hands to steady himself, and found nothing solid, and yet the fragile fibres supported him. The sides of the hollow, even the floor, curved. It was difficult to stand up. So he crouched, like a jerboa, waiting for the others to emerge.

They came in silence, except for the soft rustle their hands and feet made. The leopards came last, playing their eyes slowly around this innermost sanctuary.

There were no paintings here, no glittering lamps, no altar, no thrones. The moving light showed that ears of corn were all its gold, thistledown its only silver. Its jewels were faded flower petals and crumbling moss. And yet they felt a stillness seep into their souls, quieting their racing pulses, slowing their breathing. Their hearts were filled with the certainty that they had come at last into the holiest place. No one wanted to speak. The curiosity to look around them no longer mattered. They were content to nestle where they were, to know peace, after all their fears.

It was like waking from a long and refreshing sleep when Novan focused his eyes on Alalia's face, where Almond's eyes rested. She smiled at him. The memory of their betrothal swung into focus. Something twisted his heart.

He struggled to his feet. His hands covered his face. 'I cheated you!'

'What do you mean?'

'You don't know, Alalia!... I never told you... I nearly killed you!'

She had half risen, too, her face alarmed. He was terrified that if he told her the truth he would lose her even now. Yet here, in this sacred place, only the truth would do.

'I came to Femarrat carrying grommalan poison. It was meant for the High Sorcerer. I was supposed to assassinate Cozuman. But when I found I couldn't get near enough to him, I thought the next best thing was to drop it in the jar of wine they were drawing for him... for all of you! I nearly did it. You'd all have been dead... you... Balgo... even Mina might have drunk it. That's how much I hated the Children of Yadu. I didn't care who I hurt, so long as I killed Cozuman.'

There was a shocked stillness. Even Mina was staring at him. She had never fully understood what Novan was going to do when she cut the package out of his collar.

'But you didn't,' said Alalia slowly, getting to her feet. She held out her hands to him. He could not meet her eyes. 'What stopped you?'

'You did,' he mumbled. 'You knew my name. You treated me like a human being.'

She gave a little cry of distress. 'But of course you're human.'

'It doesn't always feel like that.'

'Then... I'm sorry too. No one deserves to be murdered, but no one deserves to have their humanity taken away from them, either. Will you forgive us... me?'

He had nearly taken her life, and she was asking him for forgiveness. He could hardly speak. Her hands had found his, and held them strongly. 'Novan?'

'I love you,' he said, his head hanging. 'I didn't think it was possible that you could love me.'

'But it doesn't have to be like we've always known it: us hating you and you hating us. Someone has to stop it.'

'Yes! That's why I was sure you had to get betrothed in the

158

pool.' Mina was clapping her hands. 'I didn't know if we'd ever get out of there, but you still had to do it, whatever happened. Digonez was smashing the paintings, so the Yadu would never know that one of their women once married a Xerappan king, or the Xerappans that they had a Yadu queen. So you had to do it again. We had to make it real for our generation. Even if it was the last thing we did.'

'I never finished the ceremony, though, did I?' Balgo said ruefully.

'Then do it now.'

Balgo held up his sorcerer's rod, though he did not light it. 'Novan and Alalia, you have made your promises. I declare you betrothed to marry each other.'

'*And may the great Jerboa keep you together in the heart of peace, and deliver us all!*'

Mina picked up handfuls of dried flowers and threw them over the couple. Novan and Alalia and Mina and Balgo all hugged each other, laughing a little hysterically. The jerboas capered around them, with joyful leaps of their long hind legs. The leopards were not given to purring, but they rubbed around the legs of the humans, caressingly.

'That was a wonderful ceremony,' cried the bride-to-be. 'Thank you, Mina and Balgo ... Now, how can we get out of here?'

Novan felt a wave of longing. Of course, they must escape. They couldn't stay here for ever. Yet, something deep in his being wished he could. In the Jerboas' Nest, everything was safe, peaceful, right.

A stillness fell over the Nest. The humans were all looking down at the jerboas, who seemed to be playing a sort of rodent leapfrog. Thoughtcatcher stopped and tilted his head to look up at them.

'*You have everything you need. The way to move on is*

here.'

The four questioned each other's faces in the leopard-glow.

'Is the way your spell-rod, Balgo?' asked Mina. 'I didn't want you to use it before, because I was sure this was a Xerappan holy place, and you'd sort of... dirty it. Yes, I'm sorry! Only now I know we're not as different as I thought we were. And if you're a sorcerer, you must know spells. Can you magic us out of here?'

Balgo fingered the slender white cylinder. 'I doubt it. I didn't do badly in my exams, but I'm still only a probationer. To magic four people, two leopards and two jerboas out from under the heart of a mountain, that's powerful stuff.'

'Couldn't you try? I'll volunteer to go first,' Novan offered. 'If it goes wrong, the rest of you can try something else.'

'Thoughtcatcher!' scolded Alalia. 'You're not helping.'

The jerboa rolled innocent black eyes upwards. Alalia followed his gaze. Her eyes widened. 'There?'

The others broke off and turned to see where she was looking. Her head was tilted back, staring at the curving roof above her.

'Are those roots?' whispered Mina. 'What tree could reach through all that rock, this far down?'

'Is it a way out?' Novan asked.

'Tree roots were our way in,' Balgo reminded him.

The leopards' eyes scarcely lit the canopy overhead. Balgo made a small white flame dance on the end of his rod. The light travelled over the arch of the Nest. It revealed an intricate network of brown tendrils, twining under and over each other in a woody interlace. It was hard to distinguish a tap root.

'It must go all the way up into the daylight, mustn't it? Do you think there are any spaces between the roots?'

'It would feel almost like trusting yourself to the tentacles of an octopus,' Alalia said quietly. 'But I think that's what we have to do. If Thoughtcatcher says that's the way out, we have to trust him.'

'How do we get up there?' Novan asked, practically.

'Stand on my shoulders,' Balgo offered.

Novan reached up his strong hands to grip two of the thicker roots. Balgo hoisted him higher.

'There's a cavity.'

Novan's head disappeared. Then his shoulders forced their way after. The roots creaked and strained as he transferred his weight. The others held their breath. They watched his legs wriggle through, and then his face reappeared.

'Pass Mina next.'

He reached down his hands to grasp her wrists as she stood on Balgo's shoulders. One swing, and she was up beside him.

'*Eh... hmm!*' Whisper's polite cough made them all stop.

'Sorry!' laughed Alalia, running to pick up the tiny jerboas. She held them aloft, one on the palm of each hand. They leaped miraculously high and disappeared up into the shadows.

'What about the leopards?'

For answer, Almond sprang on to her shoulders, and Quercus on to Balgo's. The two Children of Yadu stood prudently still, astonished, as the fur of the big cats wrapped itself around their faces. Novan widened the hole, and with two powerful bounds the leopards joined him and Mina.

Alalia and Balgo looked at each other. Their eyes shared the same knowledge. The Xerappans were above them now, with their jerboas and their leopards. They could go on if they wanted, if there *was* a way on. They could leave the two Yadu behind.

'Alalia!' Novan called, low and urgent.

The moment of doubt passed. Strong, loving hands gripped hers and hauled her up to join him.

Balgo was hardest. His weight hung from Novan's wrists. It threatened to pull him back down, though the girls clung on behind. At last, when the pain in Novan's muscles was becoming unbearable, Balgo wrenched one hand away. There was a muttered word, a fizzle of fire, and he was through. He was grasping his sorcerer's rod. After a brief grin at them, his face looked worried.

'Sorry. I didn't want to use magic unless I had to. All the rods of the Sorcerer Guard are connected. Cozuman can sense any unauthorized spells. I think we're probably safe enough down here, with the bulk of Mount Femarrat insulating us. But if this is a passage to the surface, ripples of magic might travel up it and warn him.'

'*Is* it a passage?' Mina asked.

'Yes,' said Novan. 'Feel behind your shoulders.'

'It's nearly vertical,' she called, fumbling in the darkness.

'We've got the roots to help us climb. I'll go first.'

'Let one of the leopards lead. They're good at climbing trees, aren't they?' Alalia suggested.

Quercus led the way. Soon Novan was uneasily aware that it was more of a labyrinth than a single passage. He felt like a snaking root himself as he climbed over and under the branching steps, which were growing steadily thicker as they ascended.

It was difficult to talk. He looked down occasionally and sometimes caught the faintest gleam of Almond's eyes far below him. More often, they were hidden by the tangle of roots. The three behind him were no more than heaving shadows.

'Every muscle I've got is aching,' Mina panted. 'But at least there's always something to sit on for a rest. How much further?'

'How would I know? What worries me more is where we're going to come out.'

162

They struggled on. Sometimes Novan's shoulders dislodged showers of earth, causing muffled cries of dismay from those beneath. He was following a massive root now, which led straight upwards.

'*Stop!*' Thoughtcatcher's warning pierced him like a needle. Until then he had sensed the jerboa only as a faint scrabbling not far away.

He lifted his face. He could see little past Quercus above him, but he thought he glimpsed a pale glimmer on the sides of the shaft that was not the gold of Quercus's eyes.

The others had stopped too, either because they had heard Thoughtcatcher, or because those above them had stopped. There was a tense silence.

'*Let Balgo go first,*' ordered the jerboa.

It was difficult for the young sorcerer to climb past all the others, but at last he overtook Novan.

'*Wish us good luck.*'

'Us?' Novan realized with a start that Whisper was perched on Balgo's shoulder. The two went on, squeezing past Quercus. Balgo's body blacked out that trace of light. Then the glimmer returned.

'They're through,' muttered Novan. 'But where?'

From far away came a voice that chilled them more than any other could have.

'Balgo Yekhavu! You're the last person I expected to see here. What are you doing in my courtyard?'

It was Lord Cozuman.

Chapter Twenty-One

Novan rounded on where he assumed Thoughtcatcher was. 'You've brought us up into Cozuman's house? Of all the places on Mount Femarrat?'

There was a titter of laughter.

'It's not funny! Of course, that cypress tree in his courtyard that you can see from miles away! But why? You knew, didn't you?'

'*Ssh!*'

They listened to the voices overhead.

'Alalia ran away, sir. I've been searching everywhere for her. Across the mountain first, then underground.' Balgo stammered out his story. 'Is there any news?'

'That Digonez caught you in the tunnel. That you deceived him to hide your sister and those perfidious Xerappans. That he trapped you all in the deepest cavern and then obliterated it. *How did you escape?*'

'I was on my own when Digonez found me, sir. But did you say... he blasted the caves? ... He's killed Alalia?'

'Your sister forfeited the privileges of a Child of Yadu when she insulted Digonez on their betrothal day. She deserves no more mercy than a murdering Xerappan. A wound to my nephew is rebellion against me, the High Sorcerer. It threatens the whole safety of Yadu. She got what she asked for. And so, I thought, did you.'

'It appears not, sir.' Balgo seemed to be having trouble

with his breathing. 'Digonez's report was mistaken about me. So Alalia may have escaped too. There are many tunnels down there. Did Digonez see her die?'

'He tells me he comprehensively destroyed all the ways out.'

'The Xerappans are cunning. Mount Femarrat was their sacred place before it was ours, wasn't it? They may know underground routes we've no idea of.'

'*Good work, Whisper,*' Thoughtcatcher murmured. '*Keep it up.*'

With a start, Novan realized that Balgo was not finding these words unaided.

'Those tunnels have been thoroughly mapped. All exits are guarded.'

'All *known* exits, sir. The one she and her friends escaped down had no Fence-wire.'

There was a pause. 'That hole by the bridge? But there was no ladder out of it.'

Novan remembered the drop into darkness, under the arched roots of the cedar tree. There had been no way back.

'There could be more hidden exits. I won't believe Alalia's dead until I see her body. Let me take a tracker, sir. A loyal Xerappan who knows this country and the old paths. If she's still alive, we'll find her. For the honour of the Yekhavu family, I'd rather see her brought to justice than accept that she was killed like a rat in a hole.'

'Foolish optimist. But I understand your feelings, boy. She fooled you. If I were her brother, I wouldn't forgive her that, either.' The voice was cold and cruel as jagged ice.

'I... I have your permission then, sir? To go on searching for them?'

'It can do no harm. I'll tell Digonez. He's touring the base of the mountain to check every exit for himself.'

'*A pity Cozuman doesn't know there's one in his own back*

yard!'

'I'll... I'll be on my way then, sir. It'll soon be dark.'

'Darkness is no barrier to a sorcerer, Balgo Yekhavu.'

'Of course not, sir.'

There was a long silence. Novan imagined Cozuman walking away from the cypress tree on soft-soled boots. But then the High Sorcerer spoke again, startling him.

'Your sister was very beautiful, was she not, Balgo Yekhavu?'

'So... so people say.'

'A pity. We may have to spoil it.' A low, cruel laugh that made Alalia catch her breath. 'Take this bracelet. It gives you my authority to pass through any Fence in pursuit of her.'

There was a moment's silence. Then Balgo's shocked response, 'Me?'

'I have said so.'

'Th... thank you, sir.'

This time the silence lengthened until it seemed certain that one, at least, of the speakers must have gone. But which? None of those clinging to the tree roots dared to call out.

'What are you waiting for?' Whisper's question sounded inside all their heads.

Thoughtcatcher must have impelled Quercus forward. The leopard started to climb. Novan followed, trying to stop himself from trembling, from anger as well as fear.

They emerged carefully into the twilight of the courtyard. Too late, panic gripped Novan's heart. Thoughtcatcher had surely made a fatal mistake. The beam from Quercus's eyes would betray them here!

There was a terrifying moment before he saw the truth. Outside the sacred mountain, the leopard's eyes were no longer more brilliant than those of any other cat.

The shadows were deeper under the cypress tree, where a mat of roots shielded the hollow shaft down to the Jerboas'

Nest. Only a few windows of Cozuman's house gleamed with light. It was very different from the glitter and glamour of his supper party. Outside, though, the security lights threw a brilliant glare over the surrounding hillside.

The stillness made Novan shiver. Alalia and Mina wormed their way free. Balgo hugged his sister silently.

They were standing in what must surely be the most dangerous place in the land of Yadu.

Balgo was studying something in his hand. Mutely, he held it out to show them. The silver of the bracelet hardly showed in the grey light. A single large stone glowed purple.

Alalia shuddered. 'Lord Cozuman's magic?'

'*Now!*'

At Thoughtcatcher's sudden command, the leopards were up and over the wall in one flowing movement. There was a shout of alarm from the sentries. A report and a flash of red light. An animal howled in pain.

The humans left behind looked at each other in dismay.

'*Well,*' snapped Thoughtcatcher. '*Get on with it, Balgo. They need to be invisible. Fast.*'

'I'm not sure I can do that. I'm only a probationer.'

'*Holding the High Sorcerer's bracelet? I think you can.*'

'You want me to use Cozuman's amulet? Here, in his own house? He'd know at once!'

'*I doubt it. There's so much powerful magic emanating from this place, a little more's not going to make much difference, is it? And he won't be expecting you to use it so soon. This may be the only place you can use it safely.*'

Balgo slipped the bracelet over his own wrist. The deep-purple stone burned with an inner fire. He stared down at it, at first incredulously. The High Sorcerer's bracelet, on the arm of a probationer. Then the shadowed lines of his face deepened in concentration. He turned the bracelet. Muttered words made the hearers shudder. Novan glanced swiftly at

167

Alalia and Mina... and could not see them. His own body felt curiously light and insubstantial. Balgo was staring at the space where they had stood. His arm trembled and dropped.

'*Move!*'

Recovering himself with an effort, Balgo stepped briskly towards the gate. They had to follow him. It took an enormous effort of self-control not to run when the sentry challenged him.

'Blood?' The guard called out, and waited for the second half of the password.

'... *and honey.*' Whisper had tucked herself into the folds of Balgo's uniform.

'... and honey. Balgo Yekhavu, on a mission from Lord Cozuman, to hunt the fugitives.'

'Yekhavu? No one told me they'd let you in here. You're not in the guard-room register.'

'And the High Sorcerer would prefer it if you didn't mention this in the register, either. It's a sensitive mission.'

'Too right. That sister of yours fairly...'

The bracelet on Balgo's arm crackled with dark fire.

'Sorry, son... er, sir. Should have kept my mouth shut. Pass, friend.'

It was the hardest walk, out through the High Sorcerer's gate, into the glare of the bare hillside beyond. Novan held his breath watching the sorcerers' rods probe Balgo as he passed them. But then the rods dropped to their sides. The other three crept forward.

Could the guards really feel nothing as Alalia, Mina and Novan walked between them out of the gate, following Balgo? How could even highly-trained sorcerers imagine that Alalia Yekhavu would walk out of Cozuman's own house, past their noses? They let her go.

The other sentry called, 'And keep your eyes skinned. There are two wild beasts loose. Big ones. I think I winged one. They should never have allowed those Xerappans to bring their big cats through the Fence. If I see one again, I'll strike it dead.'

It was a long, frightening way across the wide, cleared space, with the lights blazingly bright after the dark tunnels. The sentries were watching Balgo's every step. Each moment, the fugitives expected a shout to ring out, a spell to blast them, or Cozuman's cruel laughter as he sent his demons leaping out to seize them. Still nothing happened.

They reached the green steps, which tipped them over into twilight.

'Well, that went off nicely,' Thoughtcatcher observed. *'The bold approach is usually the best.'*

'You were scared stiff,' scolded Whisper.

The humans started. It was a cold thought that the jerboas could be afraid too.

'All the same, it may have been just a bit too easy.'

'How do we get you off the mountain?' Balgo asked. 'There's the fiercest Fence in the country around it.'

'The same way. Just walk through the gate. You've got Cozuman's bracelet. The magic of the Fence should disguise it. After that, it gets more dangerous.'

Balgo held out his arm, palm downwards. Though the steep staircase shadowed them now from the security lights, the High Sorcerer's amulet glowed both rich and sombre. They gazed down at it, conscious of Cozuman's authority, so astonishingly entrusted to Balgo's keeping.

'Put it away!' cried the invisible Alalia tensely. 'I don't want to look at anything of his.'

A little reluctantly, Balgo slid the bracelet off his wrist and dropped it into the pocket of his tunic. Immediately, there was a silver shimmer in the night. Novan could half see Alalia and Mina.

Balgo's hand clenched in his pocket, as though he were tempted to take the bracelet out again. 'Lord Cozuman really wants to find you, Alalia, doesn't he? Alive.'

Alalia shuddered. Novan put his arm round her. 'We won't let him.' It was strange to feel her half-seen shoulders.

'Oh, yes?' She laughed shakily. 'You and whose army? Like you wouldn't let him persecute your Xerappan people?'

'We're betrothed. They're your Xerappan people now. You've joined us.'

'And I'm beginning to find out how it feels.'

They went hurrying down the high, smooth steps. The falling night was very still around them. Novan kept looking to either side for the gold or green beam of a leopard's eyes, before he remembered he would no longer see them out here. Which one had been hurt? And how badly? It had been impossible to wait and search around the walls for a body.

'Thoughtcatcher?' he begged.

'Keep going. Concentrate. We don't want any broken necks.'

He just had to trust.

There were lights in the township where the Yekhavus had lodged. Mina and Alalia were now casting shadows behind him. Novan looked round. The evidence of his own reality was there too. He looked down at his hands. The return of normality already seemed strange.

'Can't you make us invisible again?' he begged Balgo. 'What if someone recognizes Alalia's face?'

'A spell would be even more dangerous here. Thoughtcatcher's right. If Cozuman's headquarters is monitoring magical activity, this would be harder to explain.'

They were almost at the foot of the steps now. Ahead lay the road through the township.

'I wish we could tell Ma we're alive. She must be going frantic.'

'Don't be ridiculous,' muttered Balgo. 'It would be all over Mount Femarrat in two seconds.'

'I feel like a ghost. Everybody believing I'm dead.'

Balgo drew Cozuman's bracelet out of his pocket and put it on again. In the glow of the street lamps the purple stone shone with a dark brilliance. He fingered it thoughtfully, almost lovingly.

'Maybe I should. Just in case anyone asks questions.'

The purple stone pulsed as he muttered the words. The shadows lightened where the three had stood. Once more, only Balgo was visible.

He began to stride haughtily forward, like a senior officer of the Sorcerer Guard. The others followed, walking as lightly as they could, trying not to disturb the smallest pebble to betray their presence.

The street, which had been relaxed and festive the night before, was almost deserted.

'Where have all the sorcerers gone?' whispered Mina. 'Are they all out searching for us?' Novan's invisible hand groped sideways to silence her.

There was an occasional subdued murmur from behind a courtyard wall. A small group outside an alehouse called out to Balgo.

'Who's there? Come and join us, if you're off duty. This place is dead tonight.'

'Special mission. The High Sorcerer's orders.' The purple stone flashed in the light from the alehouse door.

One of the sorcerers whistled. '*That* serious?'

'Good luck, whatever it's for! I wouldn't be in your shoes if you fail him.'

'Just a minute. Aren't those probationer's flashes on your shoulders? A special mission? Who *are* you?'

'Balgo Yekhavu... sir.'

There was an astonished silence. A ripple of uneasy

laughter ran through the group.

'*Yekhavu!* That girl's brother? ... With Lord Cozuman's arm-ring?'

'We thought you were dead!'

'Well, that explains a lot... I suppose...'

They stared at him for long moments. One of them fingered his sorcerer's rod, and put it away again.

'Better be on your way, then, lad. The High Sorcerer doesn't like to be kept waiting for results.'

They watched him go. This time Novan felt the prickle of spell-rods seeking him out. What did they sense behind Balgo? These sorcerers were uncertain, not quite satisfied. They knew there was something wrong, yet they were afraid to question Cozuman's orders.

'They didn't believe you,' hissed Mina, as they left the houses behind them. 'Not quite.'

'We got through,' said Balgo curtly. 'That's enough.'

'What if they report back to Headquarters?'

Without warning, Balgo left the road and took a path cutting more steeply downhill. For a few moments they were in shadow again. Then lights glared on a black cobbled road, a line of huts. Novan drew his breath sharply.

'The barracks? Where we slept last night?'

'More to the point,' said Balgo, 'the stables. We need to move fast.'

There was a grunting in the twilight beyond. A white bulk stirred. At a soft command from Balgo, the camel rose to its knees. Balgo was already fetching the saddle. He threw it in the direction of Novan's voice.

'Get that on.' He studied the line of sleepy camels and selected a sandy-brown one. 'She looks docile... as far as camels go. Have you ever ridden one?'

Novan and Mina shook their heads. Then, realizing he could not see them, they murmured 'No.'

172

'How are you with camels, Thoughtcatcher?'

'So-so. Give me a leopard, any day.'

As if only waiting for this summons, a dusky shape slid through the shadows. Two camels barked in fear. The jerboas silenced them instantly. The faintest gleam of golden cat's eyes drew steadily nearer. Quercus? Novan held his breath. Where's Almond? his heart was begging. At last, more slowly, he sensed another shape dragging itself past the line of softly-swearing camels. Novan ran to meet her and threw his arms round her neck.

'What happened to you?' He ran his hands over Almond's sides. With a snarl, she sprang away as his fingers touched raw, scorched flesh.

'Let me.' Balgo was beside him. 'Thoughtcatcher, can you hold her steady?'

'I'll try.'

The shuddering cat let the sorcerer approach her, though it was clear she would have fled or attacked him, if she could. His hands approached the wounded hindquarter.

This time the sorcerer's words sounded more clearly in Novan's mind. He knew beyond doubt these had the power of healing. He watched new skin creep over the burned flesh. He felt Almond relax, saw her green eyes begin to brighten.

'I didn't know you could do that,' said Alalia behind them.

'Just first aid.' Balgo rose and dusted his hands. 'All sorcerers have to learn it.'

Mina finished strapping the saddle on to the second camel. 'Ready to ride, sir.' Her voice came out of the darkness.

'Get up behind me, then.'

She climbed, a little nervously, aboard the white camel. With some confusion, since they could not see each other, Novan and Alalia shared the brown camel.

At a command from Balgo, the beasts rose up from their knees and unfolded their legs to their full height. The saddles swayed. Mina clung on to Balgo. Novan felt Alalia clasp her arms round his waist. They were pacing towards the main gate that would take them through the Fence surrounding Mount Femarrat, the most powerful barrier in Yadu and the most closely guarded.

Chapter Twenty-Two

Even the leopards were invisible now. Only the sudden starts and flinching of the camels told where the big cats flowed alongside.

They were approaching the corner where the road past the barracks joined the main thoroughfare to the gate. Balgo turned in his saddle, looking back to where he thought the others should be.

'I'm sorry, Novan. I can't explain the second camel with no one riding her.'

Novan heard Alalia gasp behind him. He looked down and saw with shock his own hands, solid flesh, holding the camel's reins. Alalia's arms briefly appeared round his waist, then vanished.

'*Interesting,*' commented Thoughtcatcher. '*But I'm not sure he's going to like it.*'

Novan was staring, not just at his own frightening visibility, but at something worse. He was no longer wearing his Xerappan clothes: the baggy trousers, caught in at the ankles, the embroidered shirt. Instead, Balgo had given him a belted tunic, not very different from the uniform of the Sorcerer Guard. Only the colouring marked it out. Where the sorcerers ordinarily wore red, or a ceremonial uniform of white with red borders, as Balgo did now, this tunic was red and yellow striped. The sight of it made Novan sick with hatred. This was the uniform given to the Xerappan collaborators. Those who served the Yadu as interpreters, trackers, special police, against their own people.

There was no time for the violent protest which was rising to his lips. Balgo's camel was already rounding the corner. Next moment, the main gate of Mount Femarrat was in view. The lights were blinding.

The guards at the Fence gatepost were tense. The shock waves of that day had rocked the whole of Femarrat. Digonez, the High Sorcerer's nephew, defied by a girl from some backwoods colony over the border. Two Xerappan traitors escaped. Their leopards loose. The sorcerers were nervous, alert for more danger.

Whatever they were expecting, it was not two grumpy camels, a probationer sorcerer and a surly Xerappan collaborator, approaching from inside the Fence.

'Blood?' one of them challenged.

'And honey.' Balgo shot back the night's password.

'Who's that behind you?'

'A native tracker. I'm on a special mission from Lord Cozuman. He believes those Xerappans will try to smuggle Alalia Yekhavu over the border. We have to get her first.' He flashed the ring with an air of authority.

'A darkie, is it? Let's have a look at him,' the guard insisted.

Novan lowered his head. The sorcerers were close and suspicious.

'Don't hold us up. The High Sorcerer doesn't like to be kept waiting.'

Balgo turned the bracelet on his arm. The sentries flinched as the purple light flared.

'On your way, friend.'

In front of them rose the enormous barrier of Femarrat's Fence. Through lowered eyelashes, Novan saw the flash of rods from either side. He felt his spine shudder with the force of chanted spells. The Fence shimmered. It was almost too blinding to watch. The trellis-work writhed like a live thing. It seemed to resent this opening in the night. The sentries muttered to themselves as the mesh contorted. Metallic fingers groped back, struggling to find their severed companions. He heard the hiss as they were forced apart again, hunching themselves into two malevolent towers, just wide enough apart for a camel to ride through. The jerboas struggled to calm the invisible, but terrified, leopards. Balgo's camel sank to its knees. It needed all Thoughtcatcher's strength to drag it to its feet again.

As the group passed through it, half seen, half unseen, Novan was sure every detail of it must be absorbed by the brooding power of the Fence and sent back to Lord Cozuman. Surely nothing could hide from the High Sorcerer who they were and where they were going? Why was he playing games with them? Why didn't he stop them?

They were out, but the Fence stood open still and the sentries watched.

They were not clear yet. There was a sickening tension as they approached that outer guard post, where they had parted from the main road to take the way to Femarrat. Novan felt Alalia shiver, remembering the knowing jokes of the sentries about the young bride-to-be. He did not dare say anything aloud to comfort her. There must appear to be nobody but himself riding this camel.

In answer to the second challenge, Balgo displayed the bracelet flashing on his wrist. He was growing in confidence. The probationer's insignia on his uniform hardly seemed to matter now. From his bearing, he could have been an officer, like Digonez.

Again, the guards whistled their surprise. One of them looked past him to Novan.

'So Xerappans ride camels now, do they?'

'I could have told you there'd be trouble when they started

letting them back on to Mount Femarrat. And look what happens.'

'Getting too big for their boots ... Papers!' the first guard snapped at him.

Novan felt the blood leave his face. He had had his identity papers when he set out. Every Xerappan had to carry them and produce them whenever a sorcerer challenged them. But would they still be in this unfamiliar belt? And how could he show them here, with his name written on them in bold, black ink? The most wanted Xerappan in Yadu, who had made off with Digonez's fiancée? He looked helplessly at Balgo.

The young sorcerer twisted the bracelet so that its purple light played over the sentry's face. His voice was dangerously quiet, as though he, not the guard, were the senior officer.

'Don't keep me waiting. Lord Cozuman commands.'

The man stepped back, as if dazed. His eyes were screwed up, as though it hurt them to look too hard at the bracelet. The camels lurched into movement again. Their hooves clattered on the stones of the main road. They were past. Novan dared not turn round, but he felt the distance between himself and Mount Femarrat widening with every step.

The camels paced through an eerie stillness. A half-moon cast sharp-edged shadows of palm trees across the deserted highway. It must be past midnight. Hardly a light pricked from the houses scattered among the fields, though when at last Novan felt it safe to turn his head, the slopes to the sacred mountain were harshly illuminated by security lights.

'*That was too easy,*' Thoughtcatcher said, for the second time. '*Almost as if Cozuman's playing with us.*'

'*There was something,*' agreed Whisper. '*When he gave Balgo his bracelet. He wanted to get his hands on Alalia. I'm sure of that. And he didn't know what had happened to her. But I sensed something else. I never knew a sorcerer with such power to hide his intentions from us. Yet I felt a kind of*

178

triumph in him. He seemed sure beyond doubt that Balgo would find his sister and bring her back to him.'

Novan lifted his eyes swiftly. Though he could not see the girls, he knew from their gasps that Mina and Alalia were doing the same.

'You wouldn't,' called Alalia softly. 'You wouldn't, Balgo, would you?'

'Of course not,' her brother rapped out. 'Haven't I got you all out of Femarrat? Why would I do that, if I wanted to take you back to Cozuman? I could have handed you over to him in his own house!'

Whisper's thought came, *'Then why was Cozuman so very sure of success?'*

'I wish I'd thought to bring us food for the journey. It all happened so fast.' From the height of his camel, Balgo leaned sideways over the stone wall of an orchard to pick an apple. He handed another across to Novan.

'What about us?' said Alalia's voice indignantly.

Even Novan started, though he could feel her arms on his waist. The invisibility of the two girls made it hard to realize that they were fully here.

'I don't know if invisible people can eat visible apples,' Balgo said uncertainly.

'Then why don't you take that bracelet off and let us appear again? It's the middle of the night. No one will see us, and there's no one for you to flaunt it at out here.'

'Flaunt it? You may not be grateful, but with the help of this bracelet, I've just saved you from Lord Cozuman's vengeance.'

Novan felt Alalia shudder behind him.

'No, I haven't forgotten,' she whispered. 'I'm sorry. Thank you.'

Rather reluctantly, Balgo eased the bracelet over his hand.

He held it for a while, looking down at its violet glimmer. Then he slid it into the pocket of his tunic.

The moonlight seemed to thicken, obscuring the rear part of both camels' saddles. Alalia's white skirt appeared beside Novan's legs. Turning, he saw again the fall of her long silvery hair. Mina's dark red dress and her black curls were harder to make out behind Balgo. A paler stirring by the verge of the road was all that betrayed Almond and Quercus.

'I wish I didn't look *quite* so conspicuous,' Alalia said ungratefully.

Balgo took out his spell-rod. He traced a figure of eight in the air, while he muttered some words. The shadows darkened further. Novan felt the warmth of Alalia's arm replaced by the roughness of cloth. He turned in surprise.

She was shrouded in a homespun cloak, which covered her betraying hair and left only her eyes glittering with moonlight. Mina was also anonymously cloaked.

'Did you do that without Cozuman's bracelet?' Alalia asked.

'I am a qualified sorcerer, in case you'd forgotten. I passed all the exams, some of them with distinction. Just because I still have to complete my probationary year doesn't mean I'm completely useless.'

'Apparently not,' she said, with more warmth of appreciation in her voice.

'Can we eat now?' Mina's plea broke the tension. 'I'm ravenous.'

They sat on their high perches in the welcome coolness of the night breeze, crunching apples. Mina held out a piece for Whisper, peeping from the saddlebag, to nibble.

'Where are we going?' asked Novan, tossing his core back into the orchard.

'Across the hills. Back into Xerappo somehow. We can't stay in Yadu.'

'Won't Cozuman come after you, if you don't report back?'

'How will he know where to find me? We're certainly not going to stay on this main road. Now, can we move? We have to be clear of the plain and into the foothills before first light.'

He kicked his camel forward. There was an alarming roar and the white animal broke into a lurching trot. Novan and Alalia shrieked simultaneously as their own mount took off after Balgo's. Novan gripped the pommel of the saddle for dear life, while Alalia clung on to him.

In a few strides the ungainly trot had settled into a somewhat smoother canter. The long legs of the camels criss-crossed with each stride, like snapping jaws biting up the distance. Farms and fields flew past in a shadowy blur.

'You couldn't have magicked a cushion as well, could you?' moaned Alalia. 'My spine's bruised to bits.'

'It's about to get rougher.' Balgo turned his camel's head away from the highway on a narrower trail. The clatter of hooves was suddenly muffled. The way was already beginning to rise.

'Where will this take us? Why did you decide to turn off here?' Novan shouted his question, but Balgo did not turn.

'He can't hear you,' Alalia said in his ear. 'And I don't suppose he knows, anyway, unless Mina's jerboa told him. We just have to leave civilization behind and trust to luck.'

'Thoughtcatcher?' Novan appealed. 'Is this the right way?'

'*Does it matter? All ways will lead to the same end.*'

'What's that supposed to mean?'

The jerboa was silent.

'The stars are going,' said Novan after a while. 'I don't know if it's morning mist or bigger hills blotting them out up ahead.'

In front, Balgo turned his head, scanning the paling countryside around them. The fields had thinned out. They were entering a rocky scrubland. This eastern side of the hills was becoming more like the western uplands where they came from. Behind them now were the lush orchards, the irrigation canals of the fertile plain. A moment's bitterness struck Novan. Why could the Yadu not have cultivated these slopes? Why had they marched over the hills into what was left of Xerappo and taken over land there for their colonies?

This is not about farming, he told himself. It's about conquest, controlling us.

Could they ever escape Lord Cozuman?

The folds of the hills were closing about them while the light strengthened. There was no path now. As the grey scree began to warm to a rosy gold, shadows fell starker, blacker, where stony ravines had been cut by brief winter torrents. Balgo's white camel seemed now a ghost, pacing more slowly ahead into the shadows of a gorge, while Novan and Alalia's sandy-brown mount blended with the desert rocks. The sky was pale blue overhead. It was narrowing, receding, as the ravine deepened.

Loose stones rattled away under the animals' hooves. A bird of prey screamed, out of sight.

'What if this leads to a dead end?' Alalia murmured.

The gorge ahead bent sharply around an angle of rock. It was impossible to see what lay beyond.

'If it's not a dead end, there's bound to be a frontier post, another Fence,' Novan muttered back.

Balgo and Mina's camel vanished round the corner. The two behind were utterly alone. It seemed an age before their brown camel swung its unhurried length round the jutting boulders. The white camel was still pacing in front of them. The stony gully angled upwards more steeply now. The cleft was climbing to the clear blue sky. There was no Fence visible on the ridge.

'Halt, or you're dead!'

A brutal shout and a clatter of stones stopped them in their tracks. The brown camel's head shot up and it snarled. The four travellers looked round in horror and bewilderment, expecting everywhere to see the uniforms of the Sorcerer Guard, spell-rods levelled at them.

There was no one ahead. On either side the gully still looked empty. The thundering echoes died into silence. Then a single clink of stone told them the sound had come from behind them.

They twisted in their saddles. Across the neck where the gorge had changed direction, three bearded men stood, scimitars raised. They were not sorcerers. Their coarse woollen robes and curly black hair showed them to be Xerappans. Yet they did not have the beaten look of a subject people under the Children of Yadu. Their teeth were laughing in their black beards, but their eyes flashed fiercely at the sight of Balgo and Novan's uniforms.

Balgo whipped his sorcerer's rod from its sheath. But even as he did so, he gave a cry of pain. The rod rang forlornly as it struck the rock by his camel's hooves. He clutched his elbow.

Another Xerappan was standing perched on a boulder a little way above them. He dangled the sling from which he had just catapulted a stone, mockingly.

'Sometimes the old ways are still the best,' he taunted Balgo. 'What's brought you into the hornets' nest, *Sorcerer*?'

From the rocks ahead of them, behind them, on either side of them, more armed Xerappans were rising, some twenty of them.

Balgo's hand moved more secretively towards Cozuman's bracelet.

Chapter Twenty-Three

'*Wait!*' Thoughtcatcher's command arrested Balgo's hand. '*Wouldn't it be better to find out whose side they're on?*'

A voice boomed from the side of the gorge. 'Novan, of Thornycreek!'

A giant of a man was coming down the hillside with a purposeful stride. His grin faded as he took in the leopards, whom Thoughtcatcher was barely holding under control. His glare focused on the young Xerappan on the brown camel. 'Aren't you heading the wrong way, lad? I sent you into Yadu on a serious mission. And how dare you come here wearing that filthy collaborator's uniform?'

Novan's heart leaped with a shock of recognition. It had only been a fleeting moment in the lamplight of his grandparents' kitchen. That bearded face, leaning towards him, his hand lifting the scarf aside to reveal these features.

'Big Knife?'

The rebel leader's keen eyes scanned the travel-stained figure of Alalia Yekhavu, then Novan's sister perched on the white camel behind a sorcerer. His frown turned savage.

'What went wrong? You didn't kill Cozuman, did you? This land would have gone up in flames if you had. Retribution. An explosion of spells like you never dreamed of. But there's been nothing. So why is *she*...' he jabbed his scimitar at Alalia, 'not celebrating her betrothal to his fancy nephew? And why is *he*...' whipping round on Balgo, 'trying to escape with you?

What's going on?'

It was Alalia who answered for them. 'I chose not to get betrothed. Well, not to Digonez. So that's why we're on the run.' From the height of her camel, she looked down on Big Knife with proud defiance. 'We thought if we made for the hills we might find a way back into Xerappo, and Novan and I...' she reached for his hand, 'would make a new life for ourselves there. And when we made him choose, Balgo decided to risk his own life and help us. So Cozuman will be after him too.'

Big Knife stared back at her. 'You, and Novan here? The daughter of the Governor of the Mount of Lemon Trees and his Xerappan leopard groom? And the two of you come crashing in here with a performing circus. Camels and leopards and a pair of conniving jerboas ... You knew, didn't you?' He bent his accusing eyes on the two jerboas. 'Did you prod him into it? Finding just this route, this gully? Big Knife's lair?'

'*Well...*' confessed Whisper, looking down at her paws modestly.

'And for what?' he roared at her. 'You'd bring the whole sorcerer pack down our secret hiding place? On us and our families? For a Child of Yadu?'

'For the Children of Yadu and Xerappo,' Alalia answered proudly. 'At the very heart of Mount Femarrat they're painted together, a Yadu queen and a Xerappan king.'

'You've been down there? You?' Big Knife glared back at her, then burst into laughter, suddenly slapping his thigh as though this were the greatest joke in the world. 'You're a bold madam! I'll say that for you. So now I'm supposed to help a Yadu sorcerer and the girl who's tweaked the nose of Lord Cozuman, am I? As if the Sorcerer Guard weren't hunting me hard enough as it is?' But he was still roaring with laughter.

'*Told you,*' crowed Thoughtcatcher. '*It doesn't pay to leap to conclusions about people.'*

Then Big Knife's eyes narrowed as he gazed still at Alalia. 'So you've been down into the true heart of Mount Femarrat, have you? And lived to tell of it? I didn't think any of the Children of Yadu would ever find that. They'd scorn to go down into the earth and the dark for a holy place. They think being higher than anyone else is what matters. So they built their black temple up on the summit. *"Look up at us! We're lords over all of you!"'* He spat.

'Can you help us across the border?' asked Balgo impatiently. 'We have to get out of here fast. If I don't report back to Cozuman soon, he's going to come after me. I never believed he'd trust me this far.'

'He doesn't know where you've gone, though, does he? You'd never have stumbled on us without those jerboas. It's seldom a Yadu patrol comes this way, and we know how to melt into the scenery until they've gone by. They'd never find this bolt-hole where we keep our families. Only a Xerappan could track us here.'

'I didn't tell the sentries at the gate my search plan. Cozuman can't have any idea which way I went.'

'I wouldn't be too sure of that,' murmured Whisper.

Novan glanced down sharply. Thoughtcatcher was hopping between the leopards, intent on keeping them calm. Whisper was sitting erect on her long hind legs, combing her whiskers.

The boy looked round warily. The gorge hemmed them in. He could not see back beyond the corner, nor far ahead where the cleft climbed steeply upwards. He must trust Big Knife's sentinels, who, he was sure, would be watching unseen from high vantage points. He imagined them scanning the sunny hillsides down into Yadu. What were they seeing?

Still, it was a relief to be surrounded by people older, more experienced, stronger than himself. People he could trust.

186

He *could* trust Big Knife, couldn't he? He thought of the grommalan powder clutched in his hand as he stood by the wine jar. In obedience to Big Knife he had nearly poisoned Alalia. He shuddered. He still had to explain to the rebel leader why he had failed.

Yet surely Big Knife would protect Alalia now that she had defied Cozuman? He would get them across the border. He must know secret ways to avoid the Fence.

'Get down off those ridiculous camels.'

There was unquestionable authority in Big Knife's voice. Even Balgo hardly hesitated before he swung a reluctant leg over the camel's neck. He lifted Mina down. The others tumbled to the ground less expertly, finding their legs as unsteady as those of sailors ashore after a long voyage.

'Blindfold them.'

'Don't be silly. We're your friends,' Alalia protested. 'We're on the run from Cozuman too.'

'Oh, I'm not running from Cozuman. Far from it. I want to kill him. That makes us different.'

Big Knife's grin flashed white for an instant. Then rough cloth plunged Novan and the others into darkness. There was not even the glimmer of light now. The blindfold was itchy and hot. The knot pressed hard against his skull.

'What will happen to the camels?' He heard the anxiety in Balgo's voice. Down on the ground, his sorcerer's rod confiscated, he sounded more like the teenager he still was. Novan remembered Cozuman's bracelet, tucked out of sight in Balgo's pocket. He wasn't sure if he wanted Balgo to use it, or how.

'Trying to disappear into the hills, and they bring camels,' someone laughed. 'Very secret!'

'Pity we can't take them with us. They make good eating.'

'What about the leopards?'

'Trust the jerboas. March!' There was no mistaking Big

187

Knife's command.

The party began to move. It was unexpectedly difficult to walk on sloping ground littered with stones. Novan heard Mina cry out with the pain of a stubbed toe, as he himself stumbled. Someone caught him by the elbow and jerked him upright. The grip loosened a little, but did not let go. He heard a current of small sounds on either side of him, the swish of clothes, the smell of breath. The blindfolded fugitives were clumsy, but the rebel band surrounding them hardly disturbed a pebble, though they were moving swiftly. Novan wanted to convince himself that they were being escorted to safety, but he knew in his heart they were prisoners, under suspicion. The way they had looked at his collaborator's uniform scared him.

It was a hot, hard climb. At times Novan had to use his hands, feeling blindly for the rocky slope in front of his face, pushed from behind. He never knew how long it would be before he could stand upright and walk again. They must have left the gully where they had been trapped and moved over its lip, diagonally across the hillside. A plunge down another terrifying slope confirmed this. He felt every step might pitch him over a precipice.

They dropped out of the hot sun into shadow. As he stumbled lower he felt the coolness of shade welcome at first. Then as they went on down and down, the sweat on his skin grew chillier. He felt he must be descending a cleft so deep the sun never warmed it.

Without warning, his escort pulled him to a stop and tugged at the knot in his blindfold. Novan could see again. Well, almost. The canyon where they had halted was indeed so tall and narrow its base must be in perpetual near-darkness.

He looked up to the distant slit of sky. The crest of the ridge which marked the boundary between Yadu and Xerappo was lost to sight now. They must still be on the wrong side of the border.

There was a flicker where the shadows were deepest. More people were coming out to meet them. They must have emerged, Novan realized, out of caves too dark for him to see. They would have melted out of sight at the sound of someone approaching. The women advanced cautiously, glancing beyond and above the newcomers, as though the habit was deeply ingrained in them to fear discovery. Then, as if at a signal that it was safe, a crowd of children rushed past the women and everyone was running to greet fathers, brothers, husbands. There were hugs and laughter, relief that Big Knife's band was home safely.

But they looked nervously at Balgo in his sorcerer's uniform, and Novan in his traitor's tunic.

Novan heard Alalia gasp beside him. He turned quickly to check what she had seen. From behind the scampering children a tall woman was coming forward to greet Big Knife. She came into the middle of the deep valley, where the shadows clustered less gloomily.

There was no sunlight to gild her hair, but it fell in a pale waterfall over her shoulders, long and straight. All the people of this community had paler skins than normal, from living in the shadows all day long, but this woman's fairness seemed to gleam with a light of its own. She might have been Alalia's elder sister.

She gave Big Knife a silent hug, then turned to his prisoners. 'What's this you've brought us? A sorcerer, a Daughter of Yadu, and two Xerappans? To say nothing of a fine pair of leopards.' She bent her hand to caress Almond's head, with a fearlessness that made Novan draw his breath sharply.

As if in explanation, her jerboa hopped openly to greet

189

Thoughtcatcher and Whisper. It was a richer brown than Thoughtcatcher's mousy hue. A torrent of information passed between them, while the woman listened. Alalia stared at this brown jerboa, and then up at the fair-haired woman.

'You're a Daughter of Yadu, like me, yet you've got your own jerboa!'

The woman laughed. She looped her arm easily round Big Knife's elbow. 'No. Don't be taken in by appearances. My name is Zelda, and I'm as much Xerappan as he is.'

Big Knife fondled her hair. 'And a good jerboa is worth more than a stinking sorcerer's stick, any day.' He juggled with the spell-rod he had confiscated, with a boastfulness that made Novan uneasy. He glanced at Balgo and saw his eyes narrow.

'Provided you listen to your jerboa,' Zelda chided. She turned to Alalia again. 'Don't judge people before you know them. It's true, almost all Xerappans are dark, like your two friends here, but every so often one of us is born as fair as any Child of Yadu. Have you heard the old story – that once this whole land, when Yadu and Xerappo were all one country, was ruled by a dark Xerappan king and a fair-haired Yadu queen? I am descended from that pair, and so is Big Knife. That's why he grew so tall!'

Alalia gazed at her, as though a fairy-tale had suddenly become real. 'Then it was true! That painting in the cave, right in the heart of Mount Femarrat. The man and the woman on thrones, with people from every nation bringing them gifts. The dark of Xerappo and the light of Yadu joined to make one family.' She swung round to Novan, her eyes shining. 'We *can* do it!'

'Moonshine!' muttered Big Knife.

The smile vanished from Zelda's face. 'It didn't last. Whatever the reality of their mingled blood, most of their children were dark like Xerappans. As these are.' She gestured to the swarm of youngsters running about the valley floor, now that the greetings were over. 'There were Yadu men and women in her court; but if they married Xerappans, the same thing happened to most of their children. So the fair-haired few were always looked on as strangers. Not "one of us".' She smiled bitterly. 'I've been stoned myself, by fellow-Xerappans, many times.'

Big Knife growled, but did not contradict her.

'Still, there was peace with Yadu then?' Novan asked fiercely. 'When they lived on their island in the Middle Sea? They must have been friends with Xerappo because of this marriage. So why would they want to invade us?'

'They grew too many for their island. They needed more land. They claimed that marriage made Xerappo theirs as well as ours.'

The word 'ours' fell oddly on Novan's ears from this fair-haired woman. It was still hard not to think of her as a Child of Yadu, but as a Xerappan like himself.

'They looked at the people of Xerappo,' Big Knife's voice rumbled dangerously. 'Mostly dark, like me, like you. They wouldn't accept that we were all one family now. Fair and tall meant you were good, important, better than anyone else. Dark and short was inferior, people who didn't matter, folk who could be pushed aside, if they'd got what you wanted.'

'Like land,' said Zelda quietly.

'And they... we... had spells.' Alalia glanced at Balgo, who was standing by himself now, within a ring of curious children. They were sucking their thumbs and nudging each other, but none of them dared yet get close enough to touch him. Balgo was fingering the edge of his pocket thoughtfully. 'The Yadu knew about sorcery, and the Xerappans didn't, did they? Wasn't that queen a sorcerer?'

'N... no.' Zelda frowned, as though that were not exactly what she meant. She had released Big Knife's arm and he strode away, light-heartedly cuffing the children as he passed, like a playful giant. She watched him go. 'Not the spell-stuff, with rods like that. Not the sort of magic that *makes* things happen, that forces people to do what you want. That's not the only kind.'

'It's discovering the magic that's already *in* things, isn't it?' said Mina unexpectedly. 'Like in the tunnel that led to the painted cave. I could *feel* it. I knew I had to find where it was coming from. And it grew stronger and stronger, right down to the Jerboas' Nest. We didn't need to conjure up that magic. It was already there. It's always been there. We just had to come into its presence, and... and... *respect* it.'

'Is that what it's like?' asked Zelda longingly. 'You're so lucky. I've never been to Mount Femarrat, let alone down to that cave, and still less right down to the Jerboas' Nest. I can't imagine I'll ever be allowed to. Not even though it's our most sacred place.'

They were all silent, remembering, or imagining.

Thoughtcatcher's warning scream split the stillness apart like a lightning bolt. *'No, Balgo! No!'*

Everyone – men, women and children – spun to see what was wrong. Balgo's uniform gleamed palely in the subdued light. But something else glared with a purple blaze of its own. He had drawn Cozuman's bracelet over his bare wrist and was twisting it fiercely. Now he could reclaim his power of sorcery over all of them. The air hummed with a stream of incomprehensible words.

'Get him!' Big Knife yelled. 'He's got another spell-thing!'

The Xerappan fighters flung themselves at the sorcerer. But the ring of children was in the way. For several seconds the men could not break through without hurting them.

'What on earth are you trying to do, Balgo?' Alalia shouted. 'Don't be a fool! These people can help us.'

Novan's eyes turned from Balgo to his sister... and

widened. Alalia was disappearing. For a moment he saw the grass and stones of the valley floor through the faint outline of her skirt. Then she was gone. He looked down in alarm at his own feet, and could no longer see them. In a panic, he tried to remember where Mina had been.

Zelda's mouth fell open in amazement. She shot out her hand and closed it triumphantly around something unseen. She gave a sharp tug, and suddenly Alalia's cloak fell, fully visible, on the ground. Alalia did not appear.

Something bumped against Novan. He felt for her arm and held on to it. They were both backing away from the confused Xerappans. Novan scanned the ground on either side desperately. A slight slither of grit and dust suggested where Mina was creeping away too. As carefully as he could, Novan edged in that direction, praying that Alalia would follow him with the same caution.

'*They're making for the stream bed!*'

The betraying voice that shrieked through Novan's mind bewildered him. Then the truth leaped clear. It had not occurred to him that Zelda's jerboa could read his thoughts too.

'*Fools!*' Thoughtcatcher was yelling at everyone. '*Stop fighting each other! It's too serious for that.*'

'What's happening to Balgo?' Alalia's invisible fingers dug into Novan's arm.

The probationer sorcerer seemed to be coming and going, now a pale blur against the rock of the ravine, now vanished completely, next, suddenly distinctly visible. The Xerappan men had broken through the children and were rushing towards him. His frightened look was shifting from the bracelet on his wrist to them.

'He doesn't know whether to use the bracelet to disappear or to stun them first.'

'I think he's finding it harder to make himself invisible

than us.'

Spurred on by the roars of Big Knife, the first Xerappan lunged out his arm to grab Balgo before he could disappear again. He was only just in time. The sorcerer vanished completely... except for Cozuman's bracelet. The stone seemed to grow in size and intensity, the arm-ring a wheel of silver from which the amethyst burned with a vivid fire.

'*Fool!*' wailed Thoughtcatcher, stamping his tiny paws. '*Idiot!*'

'What's that?' The fury in Big Knife's voice had turned to fear.

Chapter Twenty-Four

The light was changing. It was impossible for the sun to reach the bottom of the cleft, except at noon when it stood briefly overhead. Yet the cool shadows were glowing red. Big Knife's band looked around in alarm for the cause. It took only a moment for Novan to know with a sick certainty where he had seen this witch-light before. Beside him the invisible Alalia caught her breath in a sob of despair, and he knew she had recognized it too.

Thoughtcatcher was bounding up and down on his stalk-thin legs in fury. *'Idiot! Idiot! I should have known. The bracelet!'* This time he was berating himself, not Balgo.

The purple stone blazed. In the crisis, Balgo had lost his grip on the magic with which he was trying to make himself vanish and he materialized plainly. He stood, a thin young man, pale and sweating, with the fierce Xerappans gripping him. But now they themselves were gripped by terror.

It was the children who had vanished. In the first instant of strangeness, Zelda had swept them back into the caves.

The leopards trembled and growled. Suddenly Quercus sprang at the nearest Xerappan. At the last moment Thoughtcatcher was recalled to this more familiar danger. He got control of the angry leopard and forced him, shivering, to the ground. But the jerboa's round black eyes went immediately back to the sky.

Out of nowhere, Alalia's scream split the silence. 'Balgo!

How could you? You've betrayed us to Cozuman!'

The far-off sliver of blue had darkened horribly to crimson. Red shadows came tumbling down the walls of the canyon, like bloodied bats. There were yells of horror from the Xerappans. Big Knife glanced briefly over his shoulder at the half-hidden entrances to the caves. Then he caught the eyes of his trembling followers and shook his head. Too late now to risk dashing after the women and children and betraying their hiding place. The men bravely stood and waited.

A ring of crimson demons landed on the valley floor around them and crouched with eyes of fire. Leathery arms flexed. Lips curled above yellow teeth. The Xerappan freedom fighters stood helpless with horror. Hands hovered over weapons but dared not touch them. Novan, Alalia and Mina huddled together, invisible but trapped in the red circle.

'He's coming,' whispered Alalia. 'I know he is. He'll find me.'

Ruby-tinged smoke writhed from the ground, more baleful than morning fog. Out of its coils more figures were emerging, human this time, but scarcely less horrifying. The uniforms of Cozuman's Sorcerer Guard, with the purple shoulder flashes of his own special troop. At their head, stepping out of the smoke, his white dress uniform darkened by the red demon-light, was Digonez.

The leopards lay cowed, shuddering.

All the sorcerers' rods were trained on Balgo.

Digonez's eyes took in the scene. The paralysed rebels, the shivering leopards, the probationer sorcerer on whose wrist Cozuman's bracelet burned now like a terrible manacle. He smiled.

'So. A haul worth waiting for. Thank you, Balgo. Lord Cozuman could have arrested you and the girl and her treacherous Xerappans the moment they stepped out into his courtyard. As long as you wore his bracelet, his eye could see you. And each time you used its power, that magic was welded to his. I wanted to go for you the moment you left the mountain. Your sister is going to regret that I ever found her attractive. Nobody will call her that when I've finished with her. And as for the leopard boy... he'll wish it was his own beasts tearing him apart.

'But Cozuman was wise to wait. Did you imagine a novice like you could get over the border unaided? That bracelet could breach the Fence, but the whole Sorcerer Guard would know at once if it did. You had to have more devious help. Rebels we've waited to get our hands on for years. Traitors who know secret ways through the hills... *and will tell us!*'

He turned his savage smile on Big Knife, who cringed.

Whisper covered her eyes and Thoughtcatcher clutched his head, as if the jerboas were recalling how they had led the fugitives to this valley.

'I know they're here.' Digonez turned back to Balgo. His voice was dangerously soft. 'Alalia and her insolent maid and that leopard boy. *Where are they?*'

The demons took a leap closer. Their knees and elbows bent, fists raised. Their leathery wings spread wide till each touched their fellow's. The circle was locked around the prisoners. Their red eyes sparkled greedily.

The Xerappan rebels retreated before them to the middle of the valley floor, too shocked to speak. The sorcerers were smiling too, taunting them. The leopards shut their eyes and moaned softly. Balgo was shaking.

'He's still doing it!' Mina whispered. 'He's keeping us invisible. That's incredibly brave.'

'Oh, Balgo,' murmured Alalia. 'I'm sorry!'

Digonez took a step closer to Balgo. 'Where are you hiding them? You *are* shielding them, aren't you?'

Balgo was clutching the bracelet, as though he longed to tear it off his wrist and yet dare not. Digonez's eyes travelled down to the arm-ring too.

'Give... that... to... me.'

'N-no.' Balgo forced the word out through quivering lips.

Digonez raised his rod. The ring of sorcerers tensed, steeling themselves against the shock that was about to manifest itself. Slowly the spell-rod levelled towards Balgo's head.

'Give... me... the... bracelet.'

Balgo shook his head dumbly.

Alalia's fingers were digging into Novan's arm in fear. Digonez started to speak. At the first word of the spell Novan began to tremble. Mina was sobbing under her breath. This was a word of such power it was a violation of the soul to listen to it, and yet their minds could not grasp what they had heard.

Digonez uttered a second awful word. His rod was beginning to glow with a fierce white flame.

Balgo's knees seemed to buckle. He was holding himself on his feet only by the greatest effort of will. His right hand still grasped the bracelet, clamping it to his left wrist.

Digonez started the third word. His rod was a static stroke of lightning, too bright to look at.

Balgo lifted his head and stared straight at him. The stone on his wrist seemed to explode with purple fire. It changed the red glow from the surrounding demons into a horrible indigo. Digonez's rod sputtered like an exhausted firework. He dropped it with an oath, clutching his right hand as though it burned him.

In the amethyst glare, Balgo managed an astonished smile.

Immediately, twenty spell-rods of twenty sorcerers were spitting fire at him, but the power of the arm-ring deflected their spells so that they struck the rocks around him in a stutter of sparks.

'I'll get you for this, Balgo Yekhavu! You and your sister!

You think you can keep them invisible, but I know how to flush them out.'

He bent to retrieve his rod, though he held it gingerly, as if it were still hot. With his other hand he beckoned over his shoulder. The other sorcerers stepped back hastily, widening the gap between them.

The crimson demons began to advance. They hopped like toads on splayed claws. Their barbed wings, already outspread and lightly touching their neighbours', rose higher above their horny heads as their bodies grew closer to each other. The circle tightened, heightened. The towering wings cast the faces leering beneath them into blood-red shadow. The valley had been dark before, but the air was thickening now with a more horrid darkness.

'Wait!' Digonez commanded. 'Get those Xerappan thugs out of the way. Bind them. I need to question them before they die.'

The demons folded their wings back reluctantly. Their eyes gleamed with greed. Through the narrow spaces they left, the sorcerers came forward again and seized Big Knife's men. Too terrified to resist, they were led away, out of the ring of goblins.

Novan shot an eager look at Alalia, then realized she could not see him. He looked behind him at the broken ring. Could they seize this moment and slip through the gaps too, while there was still time? The nearest demon glared back at him, as though it knew Novan was there. Its eyes flared brighter and it began to rub its hands gleefully.

'Now!' At the lieutenant's shout, the thick red wings closed in a wall. 'They can't escape now, even if you could make them fly. Demons have powerful wings. When the noose tightens, they'll drive your sister and her friends into my arms.'

The goblins leaped forward. Instinctively, the invisible

three started away from them, nearer to the centre of the circle where Digonez stood with a terrible smile on his lips.

The demons crouched, waiting eagerly for the next command. Digonez moved his hand slightly. Another leap. It was impossible not to back away from their red-toothed grins, their pawing hands with hooked nails. Yet to retreat from the nearest goblins drove them closer to the further ones, and nearer still to Digonez.

Too dangerous now to speak to each other, even in a whisper.

Novan saw that the leopards were on their feet, shuddering uncontrollably, plainly visible still. Where was Thought-catcher? Where was Whisper?

He saw them then, tensely erect near the middle of the valley, where the ground fell away into a dry stream bed.

'What shall I do?' his mind signalled desperately to Thoughtcatcher.

'*Go!*' The command exploded in his head. But before he could understand what it meant, Almond and Quercus leaped into the air. For a moment he saw their spotted bodies stretched out in panicked flight. Then, with one soaring bound they were over the heads of the crouching demons and away. Even as Digonez, caught by surprise, turned, Novan saw the leopards streaking up the mountainside, the sandy gold of their pelts vanishing among the brown rocks. Spells crackled after them, but only brought an avalanche of stones rattling into the valley. Almond and Quercus, at least, were free.

A little of the weight of despair lifted from Novan's heart.

Thoughtcatcher brushed his paws together, as though one difficult task had been successfully completed.

The demons growled malevolence. They shifted rebelliously, their eagerness soured into a darker impatience to avenge this insult. Saliva dribbled from their bared gums.

The heart of that malevolence was Digonez. He glared at Balgo with even greater hatred.

'You'll pay for that. But not nearly as much as that leopard boy when I catch him.'

He doesn't know! The thought soared through Novan's mind. He still doesn't know about the jerboas. He hasn't noticed them, even though they're sitting out there in the open.

Digonez struck his arm down violently. This time the bound the demons made was huge. Alalia screamed. Digonez swung round in triumph, almost facing her.

'I do believe it's my runaway fiancée. Just you wait till I get you in my embrace this time!'

'For pity's sake!' Novan pleaded with his jerboa. 'What can we do?'

Then he knew.

The idea threaded through the darkness of his mind, like the first crack of light that reveals an opening door. He felt Mina squeeze his hand painfully, and knew that she had heard it too. A moment later, Alalia gasped. Faintly at least, the Yadu girl also had caught something of what the jerboas were telling them.

He urged his thought back to her.

'At Cozuman's party, when he made his witch-light show, we were all terrified of the demons there. But *they weren't real.*'

'They picked me up and carried me to Digonez's feet.' He heard the fear still in Alalia's mind.

'Only because you believed in them.'

It was the hardest thing to turn towards the demons. To face those leering eyes, those greedy claws, those muscular arms bunched to grab them. The goblins grinned, as though they could see through Balgo's spell of invisibility and knew exactly where the three of them stood. The girls and Novan took a hesitating step forward, and smelt the stink of carrion on the demons' breath.

They did not dare speak aloud. They could only encourage each other's wavering thoughts.

'Now,' decided Novan.

Another tentative step. The nearest goblin was towering over him, now rearing up tall, its wings shooting upwards threateningly. Behind him, Digonez's startled cry warned them he had realized something was wrong. They could not afford to look back at him. But another flash of white and an explosion of purple flame made them cower.

'Balgo!' gasped Alalia.

With the last of his courage, Novan grabbed her with one hand and Mina with the other and the three raced forward. The demon roared with glee. Its hand shot out, claws hooked. Novan was running straight at the scarlet scales of its massive chest. He shut his eyes.

He tensed for the impact, in spite of himself. For tearing talons, a blast of flame. But suddenly, it was cool and quiet, and when he opened his eyes he was in deep shadow. On either side of him he heard the girls' frightened panting, like his own.

The shadows all around them were black, not crimson.

He turned to look back. He could no longer see the red demons. Only the glow of Cozuman's amethyst lit the centre of the valley, eerily beautiful.

Digonez was whirling this way and that, baffled and furious.

'They've smashed the witch-glamour. Get them!'

Novan twisted round in shock. He had forgotten the Sorcerer Guard outside the ring of goblins. He saw them lift their spell-rods and knew that invisibility was no protection at close quarters. Those rods would sense them.

'*Down!*' The command in all their minds threw them on to

the ground. They lay motionless, too terrified to stir. Their bodies were pressed into dust and grit which would shift with the slightest movement. The first scan of questing spells passed over them. Now the sorcerers were moving, seeking them further off.

Novan lifted his head. Hope sprang. Not far ahead was a slab of rock. If they could only reach its smooth surface.

It was hard to move slowly. At any moment the nearest sorcerer might turn back and come probing closer to the ground this time.

Novan's hand crept over the rock. He hauled himself up. He was trying to be careful, but a small stone tumbled away under his shifting foot. The sound seemed enormous.

'What was that?' Digonez shouted.

'Only a jerboa,' a sorcerer's call echoed back from the cliff. 'Look, sir, there it goes.'

'The wrong sort of rat!' another laughed unpleasantly nearer them. 'Shall I kill it too?'

A blast of fire scorched the rock. It was bare now.

The three flinched with a shared horror.

'We're not playing games,' Digonez snarled. 'Find them!'

Novan felt Alalia and Mina squirm on to the rock alongside him.

'It's a cave!' Mina's sudden, excited thought made Novan peer over the other side. He saw a dark crack, hardly the width of his body.

'Could we... ?' he began.

But Alalia's mind finished the thought for them. 'The children. That's where Zelda took them.'

They moved cautiously away from the cleft and climbed the next rock. It was the hardest thing to leave that hope of safety behind them.

Still they climbed. The valley floor was dizzyingly far below now. It was risky to look down. Since they could not see each other, they had to be doubly careful, to secure their own holds and not to dislodge anyone else. Nor must they get separated. They communicated in whispers now, to judge their closeness more accurately.

Suddenly both jerboas appeared, bounding openly from ledge to ledge on free-springing legs.

'Thank goodness!' breathed Novan.

'How long... can Balgo hold out?' Alalia panted. 'And what will they do to him when he fails?'

'He's got Cozuman's bracelet,' Novan reassured her. 'Digonez can't touch him. You saw what happened when he tried.'

'You don't understand!' Alalia hissed. 'Yadu sorcery isn't like a fountain you just switch on, and it goes on spouting out magic without stopping. Once a spell is cast, it's only held in place by the will of the sorcerer. It needs hundreds of sorcerers on duty day and night to maintain the Fence and everything else. It's terribly draining. Cozuman is High Sorcerer because his will is so much stronger than anyone else's. I knew Balgo had passed his exams with distinction, but I never dreamed... you've no idea what he's doing for us.'

'But he can't keep it up?' Mina's whisper came, worried. 'Oh, poor Balgo!'

All of them thought, 'Poor us', but nobody had the heart to say it.

All this time the Sorcerer Guard was still searching the rocks at the valley sides. Their rods probed the shadows. Their bodies tensed for any reaction.

There was a sudden shout of glee. More sorcerers came running.

'The cave!' Novan exclaimed, louder than he meant. He dropped his voice to a whisper instantly. 'They've found the cave where Zelda's hiding the children!'

A groan broke from the captive rebels, whom Digonez's guards had left bound and helpless.

For a sickening while they waited for the sorcerers to emerge with a new set of prisoners, the Xerappan women and children. At last the flicker of their spell-light broke out from the cliff again, almost directly below the three. They had brought no one with them.

A ragged cheer went up from the Xerappan men. Big Knife began to lead his comrades in a defiant freedom song, until a blast of witch-fire stunned him.

Now Digonez's fury knew no bounds. 'By the lightning bolt! I'll tear off your shoulder flashes and send you all back to Sorcerer School! Do you want me to summon Lord Cozuman himself to do the job properly? I said *find them*! Well, if you can't find them, kill them!'

There was an uneasy silence below. A piercing thought galvanized the fugitives into action.

'You heard him! Well, don't just stand there. Get behind a boulder!'

They threw themselves into a narrow crevice between a slab of rock and the cliff face. There was a confusion of unseen limbs, bumping shoulders and hips. Ignoring bruises, they dragged each other down into the confined shelter.

The echo of a question floated up to them. 'Kill the girl too? Governor Yekhavu's daughter?'

'Alalia Yekhavu has forfeited all right to the protection of a Child of Yadu.'

'And Xerappans never had any rights, as far as you're concerned,' Novan muttered.

Though they could no longer see what was happening below them, the result was shattering. The ravine boomed with explosions so loud they clapped their hands over their ears with the pain of it. The light had been growing stronger as they climbed higher, yet now it was obliterated in a choking fog of grit and dust. The rock in front of them swayed. Immediately behind them the cliff shuddered. A crack ran down it. There was an appalling noise of stone upon stone thundering down to the ravine floor. Below them, somebody screamed.

The three of them hugged each other, crouched low behind the rock, which was still tottering.

Mina wailed, 'It's not just people they hurt; it's the land itself.'

Larger boulders went leaping past them. Even under the ledge, a painful torrent of ricocheting debris struck their bowed heads and shoulders.

It was a long time before the ravine fell silent. Novan raised his head to peer over the rock. As the murk of stone-dust began to settle, a tiny violet light glimmered at its heart.

'Hold on!' Novan murmured. 'Hold on.'

'Do we go on up?' whispered Mina.

'We have to.'

'No, we don't,' came Alalia's voice, shaking slightly. 'I can go back. It's me Digonez wants, more than any of you. I said no to him. I have to pay the price for that. No one else.'

'You're crazy,' Novan said. 'Do you think that would save Balgo now? He's doing this for you. For us. It will break his heart if Digonez catches you and he's done it all for nothing.'

'It's changing,' Mina gasped. 'The light's going out.'

Like a fallen flower withering in the sun, the violet glow was fading. Paler and paler, until the gloom of the dust fog overcame it. The valley lay in darkness.

They heard Digonez shout in triumph. There was a blast of white fire.

'Balgo!' There was horror in Alalia's voice.

Then the amethyst fire leaped out of the fog, vivid, unquenchable.

'So now Digonez has got Cozuman's bracelet,' Novan said

206

bitterly.

He saw the tears on Mina's grimy face. He saw Alalia's clenched hands. He saw...

With shocked gasps they all stared at each other. Balgo was dead and they were fully visible.

Chapter Twenty-Five

'Quick! Before the fog clears completely.'

They did not need the jerboas to warn them that haste was urgent.

Fear drove them. There was no reason why visible muscles should ache more than unseen ones, or visible bodies be heavier to haul up the ever-steepening cliff. But it seemed so. Mina's arms and legs were shorter than Alalia's and Novan's. He made himself wait for her to catch up and reached down a hand to help her.

'There'll be a... Fence at the top... won't there?' she panted. 'How will we get past it?'

'Let's reach it first. Digonez has got Cozuman's bracelet and he's certainly not finished with us yet.'

'What else can he... What's Alalia found?'

The Yadu girl was up ahead. Her face was flushed with exhaustion and her hair lank with sweat, but she was waving urgently to them. They could see that she wanted to shout, but was having to restrain herself.

They angled across the cliff face to reach her. She was sitting on a ledge now, turning her head to look up through a gap between the rocks, past which the other two could not yet see. Then she twisted back to smile at them.

They had almost reached her when they saw her excited face stiffen in dismay. They turned, looking behind them and down, as she was.

The fog of grit, thrown up by the blasting of the rock faces, still hid the valley floor. It was stained purple by Cozuman's amulet, like a storm cloud. But where the lightest grains still floated in the upper air, a far-off ray of sunlight reached down to gild it. The surface of this dirt-cloud was no longer quiet. It was heaving, something was distorting its layers, something writhing, humping and shifting its shape. Half the length of the valley was beginning to wake into dreadful life.

'What *is* it?'

The coil of a back broke free, oily green out of the dull purple. Another hump there, and another following.

'Is it one? Or a lot of them?' Novan breathed.

A single enormous head began to lift. They glimpsed jaws like a crocodile's, fiery nostrils. Then it sank again.

'It's got wings,' Alalia whispered.

The creature spread them. Their barbed edges brushed the valley sides with a shuddering screech.

'Is it real?' mouthed Mina.

'Does it matter?' Alalia asked. 'It can fly. And it will see us.'

The cliffs gave back to them the chant of the unseen Digonez. It sounded as though he were only a few paces below. Their minds reeled at his awful words of magic, but the final command broke clear. '*Seek them out!*'

'Just when I thought I'd found us a way to the top.' Alalia's voice trembled. 'There's a gully, as if a stream comes down from the summit in wintertime and then leaps over the edge here in a waterfall. We only had to walk up it and we'd have been on the ridge.'

'It's coming!' Mina looked back in terror.

'Show me!' Novan grabbed Alalia and pushed her to the gap in the rocks.

'It's no good,' she protested. 'It's open to the sky. That thing will see us.'

There was blue sky above them now. It had been brilliant

with promise. An anguished glance over Novan's shoulder showed him the shadow that was heaving upwards. Enormous green wings, beating with ponderous strength. Slowly, inexorably, they were hauling the impossible length of that body out of the ravine. Already the spikes on its head were beginning to reappear. At any moment the eyes would emerge and see them.

Novan and Alalia threw themselves sideways through the gap in the rocks. Mina was only one flying stride behind. They looked around wildly, searching for a cave, an overhang, anything to shelter them from the monster's all-seeing stare.

There was not a ledge, not a tree, not even a bush. Only a pebbled stream bed cutting up to the skyline. Except for one lone obstruction. A single boulder towered from the middle of the dried-up watercourse. There was still a gleam of moisture around its base. Novan longed to scoop up water to drink, but he knew he dared not stop.

The stone was tall, hunched over like a cloaked woman shielding her child. Perhaps there would be shelter in its shadow on the other side. Breath tore from their lungs as they raced towards it. An ominous green gloom was starting to invade the gully behind them.

They flung themselves round to the far side of the pillar, where the sunlight still cast shade.

The shadow of the boulder moved.

'Halt!' an order rapped out. A hand seized Novan's arm and pulled him to a stop.

He whirled round, his other fist raised to strike. Alalia gripped that too. 'No, Novan!'

His captor was dressed in the wool robes of the desert Xerappans, with a cloth swathed round the head to protect it from the sun. But the eyes that looked back at him were grey-blue, the eyebrows fair.

'Zelda!' said Alalia, to whom that fair face on a Xerappan

woman had meant more than to either of the others.

'Big Knife's wife?' Mina squeaked.

Zelda nodded. Her eyes narrowed as she looked past them. 'And only just in time. Save your questions. Just follow me.'

She ducked lower into the shadow of the boulder and disappeared. At the same instant, all the sunlight around them vanished too. The bright pebbles and the winking water were swallowed up in an evil green twilight.

'*It's here!*' Mina cried, unnecessarily.

The stone bent protectively over them.

Almost blindly, Alalia plunged after Zelda. Under the sheltering curve of the boulder the stones were wet and cool. There was a lip, a shower of pebbles, and then they were waist-deep in a damp hole. Novan ducked, feeling for a way forward. There must be more space where Zelda had gone.

'I wish we had the leopards.' Mina's voice wavered behind him.

'Or... Balgo's spell-rod.' Alalia tried to keep her voice from breaking.

'You must trust to the darkness.' Zelda's voice came from in front of them.

Novan felt wet fur brush against his ankles.

'Thoughtcatcher?'

'*If you wouldn't mind, I'll get back in your sleeve. It's rather wet down here.*'

Startled, Novan was aware for the first time that the hateful striped tunic of a collaborator had vanished with the bracelet's spell. He felt with relief the familiar embroidered cuff of his Xerappan shirt.

'Whisper!' He heard Mina's delighted greeting. He could hear Zelda starting to move deeper into the mountain. Cautiously he followed her. In spite of all that had happened, there was a lightening of his heart. For a little while he no longer had to decide, to make a choice of ways on which all their lives might hang. He must trust Zelda, as well as the darkness. Somehow she had got the children to safety through the heart of the mountain. He was thankful to be a child again, like them.

It was Alalia who remembered. 'Digonez has got Big Knife as well as Balgo... and all his friends.'

'He hasn't killed them yet,' Mina said quickly. 'They're only prisoners.'

Zelda did not answer for a little while. Then her voice came back to them. 'We always knew this could happen one day. Cozuman has so much power, and there's so little we could do. That's why we made plans to get the children out to...' She cut the sentence off short.

There was a pause, then Whisper's thought edged into the silence. *'Of course! Since you knew this would happen, it couldn't be just you, here, could it? There'd have to be other rebel groups, other hiding places.'*

'Can they help?' Novan hardly dared ask. 'Not just looking after the children. Could they rescue the others?'

Zelda's voice came low but firm. 'We knew the risks, Big Knife and I. We all did. Whether he comes back or not, I'll carry on his work. And I'll pass on our story to the next generation.'

They edged their way on in silence. The water was round their ankles now. It did not seem to be flowing steeply, either with them or against them.

Presently Novan felt an unpleasant buzzing in his ears. His chest began to constrict. He was growing sick and afraid. He could not go on.

'What's *that*?' he heard Mina moan.

'Walk on.' Zelda's command sounded further off. She had not halted with them. 'You must bear it. This is your only way out.'

'We have to walk *under the Fence*?' Alalia whispered. 'The

212

great Fence on the border?'

Novan tried not to think of that glittering, writhing barrier at the frontier post.

They forced themselves forward. Into pain, into disgust, into horror.

'Going under the wire they spun to keep the leopards in was bad. But this...' Novan retched.

'Is this what keeps us apart?' Alalia reached forward and caught his hand. 'I'm sorry! All the time I was growing up I was taught we needed this. That the Fence was good, for our protection. That you were bad people. That you'd kill us, if you got the chance.'

The horror of it still had hold of his heart. He almost *had* killed her.

For some time none of them had the strength to speak. Novan was having to wrestle with a double torture, physical and mental.

In his own private torment he hardly noticed that the bodily pressure was beginning to lift, that they could walk more freely, that they no longer had to force their protesting bodies and souls through that malignant barrier.

'I hope I never have to do that again,' Mina swore.

'I wish we could find a way to stop hating each other,' Novan said quietly.

'Go softly now,' Zelda told them.

A faint light was beginning to steal across the wet stones towards them. A gentle grey at first, then pearl, and now gilding the edges where the stream lapped against the further pebbles.

'Wait.'

She stepped from darkness into twilight, then cautiously into the dappled shadows where light danced up from the moving water. She stood outlined against a cloudless sky.

There seemed nothing but air beyond her. For a while she looked out to this side and that, then down over a view they could not see yet.

She beckoned them.

The three crept forward. It was almost as hard to force themselves out into the daylight as it had been to walk under the Fence. It was not horror which held them back this time, but a reluctance to believe that there might at last be hope. They moved as though one careless touch might shatter it.

The stream seeped from the mouth of the tunnel into a rushy hollow. Beyond, the hillside fell away in stony slopes, whose sandy-brown rocks were turned to burning gold by the late afternoon sun. A patchwork of valleys and mountains stretched away into the distance. The valleys were oddly brown, where the rivers should have watered them, while the nearer hills were clad in lush green foliage. The tops of most of these had been levelled. Houses flashed from these platforms in the declining sun, each colony guarded by the shimmer of a Fence.

'Is that Xerappo?' Mina's wondering voice could hardly believe it still.

'It hasn't changed, has it?' said Novan. 'It's still "Them" and "Us".'

Alalia squeezed his hand. 'You're wrong. *We've* changed.'

Zelda stood back. 'You've chosen a different way from us. We'll fight on. That's why I can't take you where our children are now. You're on your own from here. Where will you go?'

Alalia's hand flew to her mouth in dismay. 'I can never go home, can I? Now he knows I've escaped, the first thing Digonez will do will be to check the Mount of Lemon Trees. And Cozuman will order his Sorcerer Guard to scour the whole of Yadu and Xerappo for me. Where can we go?'

There was an ache in Novan's heart. 'Does that mean Mina and I can't go home, either? I thought we could take you back

214

with us. Balgo's betrothed us. We could get married...
properly, I mean... if you were willing to live like a Xerappan.
A nobody.'

'You're a somebody now.' Alalia forced a little smile. 'That's
dangerous.'

'You were always a somebody,' Zelda's voice was low but
fierce, 'in the eyes that matter.'

Chapter Twenty-Six

The three of them stood in the darkness at the base of the Mount of Lemon Trees. Lights blazed around the hilltop.

'Do you think the leopards will ever come back?' asked Mina.

'I hope not. At least *they're* free.'

The Colony's Fence flickered, as though luminous serpents writhed along it. It made the darkness in the valley more intense. The stars glimmered only weakly overhead.

'There don't seem to be any patrols about,' Novan muttered. 'Not using lights, anyway. But move as quietly as you can, and take great care when we have to cross the road.'

They crept cautiously forward through the scattered thorn scrub.

'It's a horrible feeling,' Alalia whispered. 'As though we were doing something wrong. All we want is to get to your grandparents' farm. We're not going to hurt anybody. It makes me feel... dirty.'

'Everything we do is wrong,' Mina told her. 'We're just Xerappans.'

Novan said nothing. He had wanted to hurt someone, very much. Could the Yadu be right, after all? Right to distrust the Xerappans, to fear them? But how else could the defeated Xerappans get the invaders out of their country?

What if we let them stay? What if that old Xerappan king and Yadu queen were wiser? What if more couples like him and Alalia fell in love? What would their children be? Xerappan? Yadu? Could the two become one, so that they would never need to fight over this land in the future?

But it wasn't fair! It wasn't equal. The Yadu had all the power. On both sides of the mountains.

A dry stick cracked under his foot, like a clap of thunder. Mina stopped short in astonishment at his clumsiness.

'Sorry,' he muttered, shamefaced. 'I was thinking of something else.'

A clearer tract gleamed palely through the scrub ahead of them.

'It's the road.' Mina peered forward.

There was a tiny movement in the shadows. Thoughtcatcher and Whisper hopped out into the open and turned their round eyes in every direction.

'All clear. Move low and fast.'

The three of them ran for the thin shelter of the bushes on the other side.

Alalia stared up at the lights of the Colony on the summit. 'I wish I could tell them. I don't know which will make my father feel worse: knowing Balgo is dead, or not knowing whether I am or not. Or maybe he would rather I *was* dead, since I've disgraced him.' Her voice rose and caught on a sob.

It was Mina who reached out a hand and took hers. Novan's own feelings were still too churned up. Alalia's father was the governor of this colony. How could he feel sorry for him?

'We're your family now,' the Xerappan girl told Alalia. 'You've got us.'

Alalia squeezed her hand, too full to speak.

They pulled their eyes away from the brightly lit Colony. Now the track to the farm looked even darker. Mina was hurrying in front as fast as she could without making a noise. She was

217

the only one who had nothing on her conscience, and that lent lightness to her feet. Behind her, Novan and Alalia had moved closer together.

'They'll love you,' Novan whispered. 'They're bound to.'

Somewhere, silent, invisible, the jerboas were jumping ahead.

'*Wait!*' Thoughtcatcher's warning suddenly arrested them. Then, '*Go on, slowly. This may not be the homecoming we were dreaming of.*'

They rounded the bend in the track by the old olive tree. It was far into the night, yet the site of the farm seemed more washed with light than it should be. The sky ahead was full of stars. No walls rose darkly to block them out. They were looking right through to where the silver-pricked backcloth met the black horizon.

'The farmhouse?' Novan gasped. 'Where is it?'

A shadow rose from the ground. 'Novan and Mina, is it?' Grandmother Luella's voice came, older than they remembered it. 'Our jerboas warned us you were coming. But we've a poor welcome to give you.'

'Grandmother? Grandfather? What's happened?' Mina ran forward. She stumbled over fallen stones.

A second figure, darkly shrouded in a blanket, caught her. The old people hugged their granddaughter.

Grandfather Tiaman struggled to laugh. 'What did you scoundrels do, back there in Yadu? Did you really kill Lord Cozuman? Yesterday the Sorcerer Guard came marching down and drove us out of the farmhouse. Then they threw the strongest spells I've seen at it. They conjured up a horde of elephants and maddened them with hornets. The beasts were bellowing in pain as they came stampeding down on our farm. They flattened everything. Then the sorcerers put away their spell-rods and went off laughing.'

'They destroyed your home?' Alalia's voice was very small.

218

'Because of me? But I bet they didn't flatten my parents' house on the Mount of Lemon Trees, did they? Even though what Balgo and I did was a far worse rebellion against Cozuman than anything Novan did.'

'No, I didn't kill him,' Novan muttered.

There was silence in the darkness. There was a question the young people dared not ask. It was Grandmother who spoke gently.

'Never fear. The worst didn't happen. As far as I know, your parents and your other grandparents have got away safely. Our jerboas gave us warning the sorcerers were coming, and what they were going to do. Even so, we had a hard job persuading your father to leave before they arrived. He'd have stayed and fought them. But we all knew how that would end. Finally, we convinced him he had to take his parents away to safety. They left just in time.'

'Where did they go? Is there anywhere safe left for us now?'

Grandfather Tiaman nodded. 'They've gone west, towards the desert. There are no Yadu colonies out there.'

'They're driving us further and further out into the sands. Soon they'll have every bit of our land,' Novan protested.

'They used to have a farm in sight of the sea, Grandfather Elyas and Grandmother Roann,' Mina said. 'We've been there. Well, almost. We saw the wonderful rich farmland at the foot of Mount Femarrat. It was theirs once. Now they're refugees twice over. It's not fair.'

'And you?' Novan asked the old people. 'You didn't go with them?'

'This is our home,' said Grandmother simply. 'Thanks to our jerboas, we saved what we could from inside before they came. And we have the stones of the farmhouse. We can build it again, as our ancestors did long ago. This land is still ours, for a while longer. They won't get rid of us so easily.'

'And I'm too old for even the Sorcerer Guard to beat me as

hard as they would have thrashed your father.' Grandfather winced as he moved.

'They beat you?' Mina gasped.

'You see? You'll never be free. If you rebuild your house, the sorcerers could do this again, any time they want to,' Novan argued.

'If I run, I won't be any more free, will I?' said Grandfather. 'I'd be handing them the power to drive me out of my home. I'd rather stay here and annoy them.' He gave a little chuckle. 'This is my freedom.'

Mina stood on tiptoe to put her arms round his neck. 'Then I'm going to stay with you.'

'No,' Grandmother said, too quickly. 'You can't stay here. They want revenge. And you...' She looked across in the starlight to where Alalia Yekhavu stood tall. She had lost her cloak. Her blonde hair gleamed. 'We couldn't hide a Child of Yadu who's betrothed to a Xerappan.' It was hard to read the expression in the old woman's voice.

'You know?' Novan exclaimed. Then, '... Of course, your jerboas. Do you mind?' At once he hated himself for asking, as though Alalia were someone to be ashamed of.

'She's finding out what it's like now, to lose her home, her privileges. She's beginning to feel like one of us.' Luella bent down, a little stiffly, and scooped up something from the ground. 'As you see, the Sorcerer Guard has left us precious little to give you for an engagement present. But we still have one secret they know nothing about. The jerboas tell me your Alalia has learned to listen for it, like a true Xerappan. It's time she had a voice of her own.'

She came towards the younger couple, holding her gnarled hands cupped before her. She reached her face up to Alalia's, and the girl bent down her head to be kissed.

Then Grandmother placed her gift in the Yadu girl's hands. It squirmed. Soft fur tickled her palms. The long tail twitched.

Alalia almost dropped it. 'A jerboa! For me?'

'*It's a dangerous world. Everyone needs an inner voice.*'

'It *spoke!*'

'Of course it did,' Novan grinned. 'It's a Xerappan jerboa.'

He hugged Luella, and then his grandfather so hard that Tiaman protested. 'Steady, boy! The Sorcerer Guard didn't break my bones, but they left some pretty painful bruises.' But only Novan's arms could express the gratitude his voice could find no words for.

'She's only a few months old yet,' said Grandmother. 'But she's a clever little mite.'

'Clever and brave and loving,' marvelled Alalia, 'to come to me, a Child of Yadu!'

'What will you call her?' Mina asked.

Alalia looked up at the stars and thought for a long time. Then she gave a little laugh of embarrassment. 'I don't think I should *call* her anything. She's a free spirit. Surely she has her own name already?'

'*Traveller,*' said the little jerboa.

The stars flashed in her round black eyes. She leaped out of Alalia's hands to join Thoughtcatcher and Whisper among the stones.

Alalia smiled at Grandmother and Grandfather in the starlight. 'You *are* free. Free in your hearts. More free than we Yadu have ever been, living in fear behind our Fences.'

'*Quite right,*' agreed Thoughtcatcher, licking the little jerboa behind her ears. '*Now, can we please get going? The dawn is near.*'

'Is it possible?' asked Mina, staring beyond the shattered farmhouse into the paling sky. 'Can we really find somewhere beyond the reach of the sorcerers? Somewhere we can make a place of our own?'

'*This* is your land,' said Alalia quietly. 'Right here where we stand. Your land and mine. All we have to find is the way to make that come true.'

Grandmother joined Alalia's hand to Novan's, and clasped them both. 'There is a way, and it's not the one we tried to set Novan on. You young ones have found it. You and Novan, Mina and your brave brother. Something our generation never managed to do.'

'It happened once,' Novan said. 'We saw the evidence at Mount Femarrat. Yadu and Xerappans together.'

'Then what are you waiting for?' scolded Grandfather, smiling. 'Off you go. And start to make it happen again.'

'But how will we know where the others have gone? How do we find them?' Alalia's voice rose, even as she took the satchel of food Grandmother was handing her.

'*Oh, dear,*' sighed the tiny voice of Traveller to Thoughtcatcher. '*I thought you said she'd learned to listen to us.*'

All Lion books are available from your local bookshop, or can be ordered via our website or from Marston Book Services. For a free catalogue, showing the complete list of titles available, please contact:

Customer Services
Marston Book Services
PO Box 269
Abingdon
Oxon
OX14 4YN

Tel: 01235 465500
Fax: 01235 465555

Our website can be found at:
www.lionhudson.com

If you want to know more about
Fay Sampson's books, see her website:
www.faysampson.co.uk